SUMMER ISLAND BOOK CLUB

CIARA KNIGHT

Love at the Coast

A Prospectors Novel
Fools Rush

Bride of America
Adelaide: Bride of Maryland

READER LETTER

Dear Reader,

Growing up, I would visit my grandparents in Merritt Island, Florida. Their home was both inspiring and terrifying. To this day, I think my irrational fear of those oversized bugs-that-shall-not-be-named developed while staying with them. Living on a canal has both gifts and curses I guess.

At the end of my grandparent's road, the asphalt disappeared into the water as if an invitation to walk into the ocean. There was a climbing tree over the water at a little inlet next to the road.

My cousin and I loved to jump off of the branches of that tree into the cool, salty water on a hot day (which was every day in Florida minus an occasional cold snap in January) and swim back through the channel to the road. Yep, I was a total fishing, crabbing, ocean-going, tomboy. I'd get upset with my cousin when he'd try to talk sense into me about my dangerous ways due to his fear of stingrays and sharks. Poor guy, there was never anyone that could stop me from doing crazy stuff.

The time I spent at this hidden little gem filled me with joy. My imagination roamed and skidded over the wave caps entering the channel. That little circle of land was my escape from reality. I believe some of my first stories were created in my head while sitting on a tree limb, dangling my feet above the surf.

I hope if only for an afternoon, this story transports you to that beautiful oasis and that Summer Island will provide you with an uplifting escape from everyday life.

Sincerely,

Ciara

CHAPTER ONE

JULIE BOONE CLOSED and locked the door to the family business, Summer Island Gift Shop. Not that there was much family left to run it.

The fresh breeze swept up Sunset Boulevard to her walkway. She stood, scanning down the dead-end street that trailed off into the ocean, and then up toward the one-street downtown area. Quiet, calm, and lonely. The way she preferred her life.

She followed the cobblestone path around back to her front garden, careful to step over the newly repaired tunnel system she'd created for Houdini—her pet ferret. Okay, it wasn't her pet, but the town's. The poor thing had been abandoned by some tourists, and the smart, mischievous little guy had become her best friend.

At the back of the building, she paused to watch the palm tree in the heart of the butterfly-shaped garden wave in the wind as if to welcome her home. The breeze made a soft hum through the fans outstretching from the trunk as if to reach toward her cottage-style home. A quaint one-story with cloud-colored siding and sky-hued shutters.

Home. A strange term now that the house in front of her stood empty, void of family and friends, excluding her adopted best friend Houdini. Three years ago, her home had been full of life with parents and husband and child. Now, the dark front window stood as a reminder of all she'd lost. Husband to the widowmaker, parents to age, her daughter to a life beyond small-town living.

She closed her eyes and smiled. The salty air always comforted her, and there was nowhere on earth she'd rather be than with her memories and with her one remaining friend. The sound of Houdini scratching at the window drew her attention in time to see a light flick on inside, startling her back a few steps. She'd never trained Houdini to turn on a light. Did ferrets do things like that? If any ferret could, it was Houdini. It wasn't likely an intruder, not in the tucked away East Coast town in Florida where there were zero crimes or vagrants. Not since she'd lived here, which was her entire life, going on fifty years.

A shadow passed by the window, capturing her breath and sending a chill down her spine, but the white lace curtains opened, revealing a smiling Brianna. Her pride and joy daughter who'd gone out into the world.

Bri waved madly and then opened the front door. "Mom, It's me."

The beauty, a perfect mix of Julie and her late husband, Joe, with his curly hair, but with Julie's silver-blue eyes. Their daughter had always been a combination of the best of both of them.

"Did I startle you?" Bri glided over the cobblestone path through the garden and opened her arms.

Julie snapped out of her confusion and embraced her daughter as if she could make her stay home forever, but Julie would never do that. She'd never interfere with her daughter's life. "What are you doing here? You just went back a few days ago. I wasn't expecting to see you again so soon."

Bri slid her arm around Julie's back and guided her into their cottage. "I decided to come home. Sorry I didn't call ahead, but I wanted to surprise you."

"Why?" Bri plopped down on the periwinkle sofa and kicked her feet up on the old sea-drift wooden table Joe had made for her on their tenth anniversary. They'd had a good life together, hadn't they? Julie settled by her daughter's side. Houdini rushed onto her lap, turned once, and settled for a good pet.

"Mom, you haven't changed a bit. Hello, anyone home? It's your fiftieth birthday in a couple weeks, so I thought I'd come spend my vacation with you."

"You already took your vacation days to be here last month."

Bri patted the seat next to her. "Tell me... What're your plans for your big 5-0?"

Julie knew her daughter well enough to know she was hiding something but decided to give her space for now. She'd never been the meddling mother type, so she wouldn't start now. "Don't have any, really. Work, I guess."

Bri huffed. "Mom, tell me you're not spending all your time running that shop you don't even like." She shoved from the couch, causing Houdini to bolt from Julie's lap and run up the shelves lining the room, where he liked to sit and watch everything from a perfect vantage point. "Let's see what you've been working on. I'm always bragging about the amazing artist my mother is. Total creative type that I wish I could be." Bri pointed to the back door that led to Julie's office-turned-storage shed.

Houdini whined at the thought of being abandoned.

Wind rattled the mesh grates outside the old-style slat windows. She would've updated them years ago, but they were good at keeping out the bugs, especially the icky roaches, better than the modern screens. Besides, the greenish glass was artsy and vintage.

Bri paused at the hallway. "Come on. Show me what you're working on." She disappeared into the kitchen, causing Julie to hurry from the living room and Houdini to race undoubtedly to Julie's bed to pout. A hint of anxiety whittled its way through her nerves. She'd lied to Bri to get her to return to work a few weeks ago, claiming she would be working on her art again and would be distracted. It had been the only way to free her daughter so she'd leave. She'd spent way too much time here since Joe's passing three years ago.

"Wait, I don't have anything finished." She raced after her daughter, but by the time she'd caught up to Bri, she'd already entered the shed.

"What?" Bri turned in the center of the room, the only place left to move with Joe's things stacked to the ceiling. "I don't understand. You said you were working on pieces again, sculpting and putting together art, maybe even doing some sketching."

Julie wanted to change the subject and quick. "I haven't had time to clear out the shed. Honestly, I'm not sure what to do with all this stuff." She braced for her daughter's scolding about how Julie was stuck in the past and needed to live in the present, but to her relief, there was no reprimand.

Bri shrugged and smiled. "No worries. We can clear this out together and get your studio set up. It'll be fun."

Julie couldn't hold in her question any longer. "Tell me the truth. What are you doing back here?"

The cry of a seagull above echoed through the shed, but Julie remained with her motherly staredown firmly planted on her daughter.

Bri ran a finger along the dust-covered camping lantern, leaving a clean trail. "I needed a break. I miss you, and I miss dad. I—I quit my job, and I'd like to come home for a while if you'll have me."

In that moment, Julie saw pain flash over her daughter's face, something Bri would rarely allow Julie to see. Instead of further questions and drilling into her thirty-one-year-old daughter about wanting to give up her career and come home, she opened her arms and pulled Bri in for a hug. "Of course, darling. This is and will always be your home."

They stood there in the old shed, Julie torn between the joy of her daughter's return and the fear she would remain too long until she forgot who she was—a feeling Julie knew well. She wanted more for her daughter. It was her job to show Bri how well she was doing and lift up her daughter so that she could go back to her own life. For now, though, she'd give her some space until she was ready to talk about what had brought her home, beyond caring for her widowed mother.

Bri hugged her tight and then released her, turning away and eyeing the pile of old clothes in the corner. "We'll start tomorrow so we can get this place ready for you to create again. I always love watching how you take crazy and make it beautiful."

Julie froze. That was a saying she used to hear often years ago, but Bri wouldn't know about that. She'd never met her childhood friends. Sure she knew about them and the mischievous activities of Julie's youth with her BFFs, but she wouldn't know that saying. A coincidence. It had to be. "Let's go inside and get some dinner and chat about what's going on in your life."

Bri glanced around the space one more time. Julie knew she couldn't get rid of anything, not now, not ever, not when it was all she had left of Joe and their lives together. But that was a problem for another day, so she flipped off the light and closed the door.

"Nice deflection, but okay, I'm game to focus on me for a few. I've got some news to tell you anyway."

"What's that?" Julie knew her daughter had been dating a boy for almost a year, but she had yet to meet him. Her daughter had sworn it was nothing serious, but perhaps something had changed. Bri had never even mentioned marriage, perhaps because Julie always warned her against getting married too young. Now that Bri was over thirty, Julie worried she'd warned her one too many times, but she'd always wanted more for her daughter than what she and Joe had together in their lives.

"Nope. Not now. Over dinner. Come on. It's been forever since we've cooked. What shall it be? A soup made of anything we can find in the fridge and cabinet, or an anything taco?" Bri took Julie's hand and guided her away from the storage of souvenirs of a past life and into the home of memories.

"Was I always so scattered in life? I hoped that your dad's sensible, more organized side balanced your upbringing." Guilt pinched her like a crab, quick and unexpected.

Bri removed a bunch of veggies from the hanging basket in the kitchen and tossed them on top of the cutting board Joe made that Julie had etched a recipe into. They'd worked well together all those years. Best friends for life, they'd always said. Not big on romance, but the partnership was there.

"Mom, I was lucky to have you both. When I went away to college and I was chatting with all those northern folks in Georgia, I realized how unique a life I've had. It made me appreciate this place even more. And as for you? Ha, perfect. You made life fun and exciting and unpredictable, while Dad made it safe and, to be honest, a little boring." Bri retrieved some more vegetables from the crisper in the old white fridge. "Not that I'm complaining about Dad. Boring is good sometimes. I grew up calm, well-adjusted, and loved. I only wish I had your talent."

Warmth like a summer breeze flittered over Julie's skin through the open window above the kitchen sink. "You do, darling, and more." She tucked Brianna's ringlet brown curls behind her ear, admiring the thickness and wildness of her hair. "Is everything okay? I'm here for you if you need anything."

"I know, Mom. You're always there for everyone else. I heard from the Small-Town Salty Breeze line that you painted Nancy Watermore's fence, made and delivered food to Cranky Mannie, and cut Old Lady Francie's yard. All last week."

"Please. The STSB line has been dead for years."

"No, it's alive and well, and I'm still connected, even from over five hundred miles away." Bri peeled the onion and minced it with precision. Then diced some green peppers and mushrooms.

"Is that why you quit your job and came home?" Apparently, Julie couldn't hold in her mothering too long.

"Hand me that onion." Bri pointed, ignoring her mother's question.

Julie leaned against the counter and watched her daughter create an amazing meal without a recipe. "Hon, you can tell me anything."

"I know, Mom, and I will when I'm ready." Brianna poured some coconut oil into the pan along with the fresh veggies. Julie recognized her daughter's move as her avoiding-the-truth evasive action. "Let's concentrate on your birthday for now."

"I'm looking forward to a quiet, dignified fiftieth at home with my daughter and her amazing cooking."

"How about a not-so-alone fiftieth?"

Julie picked up the dish towel and snapped it at Bri. "Spill it. I know that look. You're my daughter. You're up to something no good."

"What? Me? I'm innocent." Bri grabbed a spatula and moved the colorful chopped and minced food around in the pan.

"As innocent as when you glued Cranky Mannie's gate shut? Or how about when you poured half a jar of salt into your dad's beer, or when you put the bucket of seawater over the storage room door at the shop? I think I should've never mentioned my youthful antics to you. I think it inspired you too much." Julie snapped the towel again.

"Ouch. Hey, dangerous. Hot pan here." Bri changed the subject and focused on tossing some chicken into a pot of boiling water. Julie had no idea what they'd be eating, but knowing Bri, it would be delicious.

"Confess, then." Julie tossed the towel onto the old tiled countertop and crossed her arms over her chest. "Are you avoiding a problem of your own? Work? Boyfriend? Or are you up to something here?"

"I'm not up to anything." Bri had a third pan on the

stovetop and was working on some sort of sauce that was a pretty peach color. "As for my job, I resigned because it was just that, a job. It isn't my passion." Bri paused her hand mid-stir. "I just think it's time for you to move on, and I hope a little special birthday celebration will kick start you into a new life."

"A new life? I'm turning fifty, not twenty-one. And I like my old life. All the wrinkly, hot power surging, sun-spotted years of it."

"Puh-leeease. You look amazing. I only wish I had your hourglass shape and those lips. I'd have to use five syringes of lip volumizing injections to make mine look like that. Besides, you look better in a bikini than any woman I know."

"Bikini? Ha. I haven't worn one of those in a decade or two." Julie held up both her hands. "If you're here for some misguided notion that I need a life intervention, you can forget it. Don't need it. I'm happy. You should go back to your life and stop butting into mine."

Bri turned down the burner to a simmer and wiped her hands. "Are you, Mother? Truly happy? Not the I-will-bury-my-sorrow-by-helping-others happiness?"

"Since when is it a crime to help your neighbors?"

"It's not, unless you don't have a life beyond that." Bri strained the chicken from the water and added it to the frying pan. Sizzles erupted. Five-star restaurant kitchen aromas filled the small space, making Julie's stomach growl.

"See, you need me." Bri pointed the spatula at Julie's belly.

"I always want you, baby girl, but I don't need you to abandon your life to come spend my birthday with me. Is that why you left your job? Did you get fired for taking too much time off?"

"Mom, I wasn't fired. I left. My choice, not yours, so let me figure this out. As for you, I know you want your old life, and Dad, but you can't have that." Bri plated the food, pouring sauce over it in a beautiful corkscrew pattern. She placed the pan on the stovetop and turned to Julie. "Mom, I love you, and that's why I'm here. Dad wouldn't want you to be alone anymore. I think you should sell the shop, start creating again, and date."

Julie let out a sound like a slowly leaking balloon.

Houdini tore through the house, into the kitchen, and up onto her shoulder, nuzzling her the way he did when he thought someone was upset. She scratched his head, and he purred in her ear.

"And Dad wouldn't want you to give up your life to come home and look after me. I'm fine the way my life is. I'm happy."

Bri smiled, an I've-got-a-secret-I'm-bursting-to-share smile.

"What?" Julie's muscles tightened in warning. "No. You're not setting me up with someone on a blind date."

"No. Of course not." Bri grabbed both plates, sat at the bistro table, and handed Julie a fork. "Sit, eat, enjoy. Let me take care of you for a change."

Julie placed Houdini on the ground and sat across from Bri. "I told you I don't need taking care of. Besides, I want you to go live your life. How's that boyfriend of yours?"

"Gone," she said matter-of-factly and scooped up a bite of veggies.

"What happened?" Julie asked.

"Nothing. Just wasn't right." She shrugged, as if discussing the weather instead of her life.

This had to stop. Bri needed to focus on her own life and forget about Julie. "You don't need to worry about me. There's nothing wrong with me and the way I live my life. You need to start concentrating on your own future."

"I knew you'd say that, but it isn't just me." Bri snagged her purse from the couch and returned, handing her an envelope.

"What's this?" Julie eyed her daughter's handwriting on the front of the envelope.

"Open it." Bri took a large bite, but Julie wasn't hungry all of a sudden.

She opened the first envelope and read the single sheet.

All call to Summer Island Book Club, January 14th.

Julie shook her head. "I don't understand." The words were hollow because her brain was processing a thirty-two-year-old message. The last time she'd seen those words, she was graduating high school. All her friends had moved on with their lives, leaving the slow, dyslexic, artsy girl behind to marry young because that was her only choice. Not that she regretted her years with Joe, not at all, but she had envied her friends' worldly lives after graduation. Kat went Ivy League. Wind landed a part in a Broadway production. Trace joined some world-renowned ocean conservation company and made headlines cleaning up oil spills and inventing new ways to combat the plastic problem in the oceans.

Julie had stayed in the same town, doing the same thing, for three decades. "No," she mumbled under her breath. "I don't want to see them."

Bri's joyous expression folded into a frown. "But Dad used to always talk about how you and your high school friends could do anything together. That you were a girl powerhouse like this town had never seen. And no matter what, you all would drop everything to meet at your Friendship Beach for book club and anytime someone was in need."

"That was then. They wouldn't care now." Julie's hands

11

trembled. To face so many successes while facing her own lack of living was too much. Not to mention they would never give up their lives for a childish notion of some female bonding time. "No way they'd show here. Please, tell me you didn't send this to anyone."

"I sent them to all of your friends, Kathryn Stein, Wendy Lively, and Trace Latimer."

Julie shoved from the table and held her head as if it would lift from her body to escape the embarrassment of a pathetic attempt to reunite an old tradition that no one cared about anymore...Except her. She walked to the window and lifted the lace curtain, feeling the rough fabric between her fingers. Clouds must've rolled in, covering the moon, because the world seemed even darker than normal. "They won't come."

The chair squealed against the tile floor, and Bri approached. Three unopened envelopes were held in front of Julie. "They answered the call."

Julie took the envelopes, recognizing the top message's handwriting as Trace's. The old friend she'd only spoken to via birthday and Christmas cards would never drop everything to come home for Julie's birthday. Did she want to face the embarrassment of rejection? Yes, if it meant getting Bri to see the error of her ways and return to her own life.

Julie slid her finger under the lip, and it snapped free as if barely sealed. Her pulse quickened at the idea of having her old friends around her, yet fearing it all at once. She opened the paper and read:

It is my honor to answer the call of the Summer Island Book Club.

Tears pooled in Julie's eyes at the thought of seeing her once closest friend again after all these years. If anyone would answer the call, it would be Trace. The others were never going to come. Last Julie had heard, Wind was on tour as a world-famous choreographer now, so she opened Wind's envelope next. In swirling letters, as if she'd written it in calligraphy, it showed the same exact words that Trace had written.

It wasn't possible. They hadn't seen each other for over half their lives, despite her invitation during the holidays the first few years after they had left. By the third year, she'd given up and focused on her own family and let her childhood friends go.

Kathryn's was last. The one who was born for greatness with a silver spoon in her mouth that her mother had shoved down her throat repeatedly as a kid. Apparently it had worked, though. She owned a law firm in San Francisco last Julie had heard. To her shock, she opened it to find the same message.

"So?" Bri asked from behind her.

"They're answered. All of them." Julie crumpled into the sitting chair by the front door.

Bri knelt in front of her. "Mom, what is it? I thought you'd be happy to have some time with old friends."

"Yes and no." Julie scanned her humble home. "I don't know that I want my life overanalyzed and criticized. We were friends, but I was never like them. They've accomplished so much in their lives."

"So have you." Bri clasped her hands tight. "You raised me."

Julie cupped her daughter's cheek. Bri was her best creation. Nothing could ever compare to her. Maybe that's why she'd given up on her art all those years ago.

"Mom, I know that you feel stuck. That you can't move forward. That's why I'm here. I know it's scary, but you need to wake up. You've forgotten who you are. Dad said you were the best artist in all of Summer Island, Florida, if not in the world." Bri squeezed her hand. "Do you know what Dad's greatest regret in life was?"

Julie blinked, fighting her fear to ask but needing to know. "What?"

"That you never lived up to your potential because you would never turn your back on your family. You spent years utilizing your art skills in combination with Dad's wood-working. When he passed away, you stopped creating anything. You stopped being you."

Julie knew Bri had a point. She *had* fallen into a rut. "But I'm going to be fifty. It's a little late to start dreaming now."

"Who says? They say fifty is the new thirty." Bri pulled her to stand. "You're the most amazing woman I've ever known. Take a chance, Mother. You're healthy, beautiful, and kind. And I believe you have something inside you that needs to come out. It's time for you to be you again."

Julie sighed. Sighed because despite the truth of it, she had no clue who she was beyond mother, wife, daughter, store owner. Who was she now that everything had changed?

CHAPTER TWO

THE FLORIDA MORNING sun erupted the heat on the back of Trevor Ashford's sunburned neck like a flare gun to kindling. After three hours hovering over the old diesel engine, his temper raged. He gripped the wrench tight, hooked it to the stubborn bolt, and turned with all his remaining strength. His hand slipped and he fell forward, sliding his knuckles against the rigid, rusted, ragged metal support beam, slicing his skin open.

He cursed like a sailor he wished he was, snatched the wrench free, and spiked it like a football in the end zone. Unfortunately, it didn't stop at the end of the deck and tumbled down the sugar scoop steps, over the back of the boat, and plunked into the salty, brackish water.

With his energy drained, he fell back against the hull. He closed his eyes to shield them from the relentless light and grappled with his insane decision to move from the Northwest to the Southeast, all to escape his ex-wife and the constant attention she brought with her.

"You know, you could hire someone to fix that for you."

His friend, Dustin Hawk, leaned over the side and held a cold beer in front of him. "Thought you might need this." Then he handed him a bottle of water. "And this."

"Thanks to both." He took the ice-cold beverages and held one to his cheek and the other to the back of his neck, hunching over in defeat. "You're right. If I had the money."

"You would if you hadn't let that evil witch of an ex take you for everything. You were only married for seven years. She wasn't entitled to alimony." Dustin climbed aboard and settled on the sugar scoops next to him, eyeing the sixty-five-foot mast on Trevor's newly purchased old catamaran. "Wait, that's right, you gave her everything in your midlife/divorce crisis."

Trevor set the beer aside, unscrewed the cap on his water bottle, and took a swig. The cool, fresh water soothed his throat. Too bad it couldn't soothe his wounds. "I didn't want any souvenirs. I'm not the sentimental type." Or reminders of her having an affair with his assistant—a man he'd hired so he didn't have a female in his office in order to soothe Marsha's jealousy.

A welcomed breeze swept through the tiny two-dock marina as if to promise a little relief from his bad decisions.

"More like you don't want to look at any reminders from the hell that crazy woman put you through. I'm not one to say I told you so, but…"

"You are exactly the type to tell me that," Trevor laughed. His best friend since high school had warned him about Marsha, his then-wife-turned-cheating-lingerie-model. "You told me she was the dating, not marrying, kind."

Dustin raised his own beer in the air. "Here's to freedom and a new start."

"How many times are we going to toast to freedom since my divorce? I think this makes about ten dozen."

"However many times it takes for you to move on." Dustin took a swig and set his beer down on the deck between them. "Not sure I made the right choice pushing you to leave your old job and life to take a break. Of course, my evil plan was to have you come work for me in the end."

"No, you were right except for the working for you part. Not happening." Trevor scanned his motorboat, his sailboat, his shack of a place, the abandoned old motel down the beach, and the docks. "I just decided to follow a stupid passion and waste most of the money I had left on this place. I should've followed your advice and found a sports car and a young woman. To date, not marry. I guess the tabloids were right… I'm a sugar daddy chasing his youth."

Dustin laughed so hard he nearly fell overboard but grabbed the dinghy davits to stay put. Once upright, he took another drink.

"It isn't that funny." Trevor wrapped his knuckles in a dirty rag and swiped the blood from the deck with his other palm. He'd have to scrub the boat later anyway if he ever had any clients to take out.

"Sorry, I had a visual of the uptight, moral, practical, business-savvy man I know acting like a midlife stereotype. You are many things, but you are not a cliché." Dustin pushed up onto his hands and knees and studied the engine bay.

Trevor eyed his friend, who was clinging to the hatch as if it were a life preserver. "You do realize you are on a boat that is floating on water, right?"

"I know. How could my best friend want to move onto the ocean? The one place I despise."

Trevor shot up and pointed behind him. "I think I see a fin over there."

Dustin glowered at Trevor. "Funny guy."

"You know, I can get you over your fear of sharks. I'll take you on a dive with me."

"No thanks, Dive Master Ex-Best Friend." Dustin returned his attention to the engine and away from his phobia. "Now, let's see if we can fix this old motor. We're men, right? It's in our DNA."

"Spreadsheets, marketing analysis, and business meetings are in our blood. I think the mechanical gene missed both of us," Trevor complained, but he wanted to fix the engine himself more than anything. He'd spent hours watching YouTube videos and reading forums. It took weeks, but he knew all the parts of a diesel motor, how to change the oil, check filters, but he knew the basics weren't going to cut it with this engine.

"Come on. I didn't use up all my vacation time to watch you give up. I'll make some calls and see if we can get someone out here to tell us what needs to be done." Dustin stood and pulled his phone from his shorts pocket.

"No need. I know what needs to be done. I'm just not sure I can do it myself." Trevor grabbed the beer and the water and eyed the sheets threaded through the cleats and wenches, trying to come up with a plan.

"What's that?"

"I'll have to rebuild the engine." Trevor lifted his chin, snapped the tab on his beer, which made a *tsst* sound, and then chugged a few gulps of refreshing, relaxing, cool, fresh wheat taste. "And I'm going to do it myself."

"Seriously? Do you remember what happened when we tried to fix your grandfather's old Chevy?"

"That was different. We were teenagers who didn't even know how to drive. I can drive cars and sail boats now. Heck, I can even sail this one if any tourists ever arrive." Trevor eyed the little two-story shack he slept in that doubled as his office. "I'm going to do this."

"I guess I better ask for some more time off. You're going to need all the help you can get."

Trevor quirked a brow at him. "You own the company."

"Darn. I'd hoped you'd forgotten that part so I'd have an easy excuse out of this job." He pushed up his nonexistent sleeves and eyed the water. "Can we work on land, though?"

Trevor clapped him on the back. "Sure, once I rig a pulley system to get the engine off the boat."

"Fine. If you really need to rebuild this grease and metal blob yourself, then I'll help, but if you change your mind, I'll hire the repairman myself. It would be worth the money to get this thing running and get you out on the water like you'd planned so you can have some time off to get some beach days with bikini-clad babes."

"I don't think there are many hotties on Summer Island this time of year. I only said that so you'd come down and offer free labor."

Dustin took another few gulps of his beer and then set it on the transom. "You think I didn't know that? Despite knowing the truth, I came. That means I deserve the best friend award for backing your crazy, especially when it comes to the ocean."

Trevor was thankful to have a lifelong friend like Dustin, even if he was a wild card and an effort to deal with at times, with his girl-hopping and overconfident ways. The way Trevor had been before he'd met Marsha and married her. She'd tamed him. Little did he know, she wasn't relationship broke herself. He'd done plenty wrong, too, though. He should've supported her modeling career instead of trying to make her stay home and play house and support him all the time. "Thanks, man. I do appreciate it."

"Don't mention it. I'm only here for the free beer and to see young girls in bikinis." Dustin sat by the toolbox and handed Trevor a screwdriver, as if that would fix everything.

"Sorry. When I bought this place, I assumed the Florida beaches were always packed. Since the cape closed across Banana River, Summer Island has lost major business with the locals moving away and the housing market tanking, but it only needs time to adjust and become a tourist destination alternative to crowded Cocoa Beach. I'm just getting in early, which meant I could have waterfront property for a steal. Don't worry. Where there is water, spring breakers will come. This little island might be small, but it has potential."

"Yeah, potential for a person to come to die. You do know you're not eighty and you could have a social life, right?"

"I know I can. I just don't want one." Trevor opened the cockpit locker and found some extra lines and blocks. "I just don't want to be social. It's a waste of time and energy, and right now, this place takes all of that and more."

Dustin stood, eyeing the water and keeping a tight grip on the stainless steel davits. He really was a good friend. The best. If only women could be more like him—dependable, honest, strong, and fun. Someone he could work beside for hours and not have to talk about feelings all the time.

"You know, I could work on that old hotel while you work on the engine," Dustin offered, obviously in hopes he could get far from the ocean and the creatures under the surface. For the bravest, most accomplished person Trever knew, Dustin's irrational fear of the ocean was amusing.

"Nice try. That old hotel isn't part of my business plan. You're the resort and rental property guy, not me. You should buy it from me and start a resort. We could work here together."

Dustin laughed. "There are limitations on our friendship. There's no way I'd ever give up my city life for some remote oceanfront, shark-infested, broken-down location. Thanks, but no thanks."

The ocean breeze brought fresh, salty air, and Trevor couldn't understand his hesitation. "You mean peaceful, sunny, warm, and a quiet opportunity to reflect?"

Dustin grabbed a rope and tied a bowline like Trevor had taught him. He didn't want to tell Dustin they needed a figure eight stopper knot instead. "You have your breakdown. I'll keep my life going in Seattle until you return."

Trevor halted his work and sighed. "You still think this is a phase, don't you?"

He shrugged. "I can hope."

And he knew Dustin did wish that Trevor would come to his senses and return to Seattle, but there was no way he'd give up on his lifelong dream of living on the ocean and running boats for a living. Okay, he was on the waterway to the ocean, but close enough. Nothing would agitate him enough to give up on his new charter company.

After a few hours of removing the engine and working on disassembling parts, carefully labeling and laying out the pieces on blankets, Dustin convinced Trevor to take a break for lunch. Despite the sun shield they worked under, the heat left them exhausted and in need of a break. Lunch didn't take long, but Trevor found himself dozing in the chair, and before he realized it, an hour had passed.

He shot up from his chair, determined to figure out the issue and put the engine back together by the end of the day.

Dustin peeled himself off the couch and hobbled toward the door. "You owe me a night out when we're done." He opened the glass sliding door and halted, standing stone still, looking out toward the ocean, which obviously frightened him.

Trevor laughed. "You know a shark can't sprout legs and walk up on land, right?"

"I don't think sharks are the problem." Dustin stepped aside. "Do you have large rats that steal engine parts?"

Trevor shot through the glass sliding door, catching his knuckles on the edge, sending a sharp pain deep into his hand. Outside, he spotted a long, thin, furry creature that looked like a weasel. It stood on its hind legs, held up a bolt from his engine, and if Trevor didn't know better, he'd swear the creature smiled at him and then took off with the piece held in his teeth. "Get him."

They both tore through the sandy grass sprouts and over to the side yard. The weasel raced toward a pipe. Trevor dove to catch it, hoping it didn't have rabies, but all he grasped was air between his hands and sand between his teeth before the creature disappeared into the pipe. He spit the grains from his mouth and scurried to his feet, kicking sand up at a protesting Dustin.

He pointed ahead. "It goes that way."

Trevor kicked off his flip-flops to get more speed and raced down the beach to a road that dead-ended onto a small beach. He hung a left. His feet pounded against the abrasive, searing asphalt, burning the soles of his feet and cutting his flesh.

"I don't think it's a pipe. It looks like a PVC wood, and wire mesh man-made tunnel," Dustin shouted.

The weasel stuck its nose through some of the mesh, as if to make sure they saw him, and then took off again. Was the creature mocking him?

An old lady sat rocking on her porch with a man using a cane standing by her side. She pointed at Trevor, and the man pounded his cane against the old wooden decking and laughed. Trevor waved at them, and they reciprocated.

"That shop there. It ran through the side of the building." Dustin took off, and Trevor followed on his heels, jumping around with each jagged shell or rock piece that gouged into his skin, knowing he was putting a show on for the residents.

Hopefully he'd hit the bottom of that ocean pit that Dustin said he'd dug for himself. At this point, he believed his friend was right. What else could happen? Nothing could top a stealing, mocking weasel-like creature that stole a part to an engine he couldn't fix to run a boat he didn't have any customers to sail off into the sunset.

CHAPTER THREE

JULIE STRAIGHTENED the old merchandise that screamed tourist junk and thought about making a few changes to the store. Maybe Bri was right. Perhaps it was time to find herself again, if for no other reason than to show everyone she was fine. That way, Bri could return to her own life instead of coming home to look after her mother. She didn't need her old high school friends to come rescue her, either.

How pathetic they must think she was, receiving a message to return for some over-thirty-year-old teenage vow. She tried to shove off her mood, but the idea of facing her friends and their sympathy didn't cheer her up the way her daughter had probably planned. A friendervention was the last thing she needed.

Houdini shot through the side door, up the plank ramp, and into the hole he always hid in when he was naughty. "What have you done?" She abandoned the display and stood below the opening to his hideout, waiting for his little nose to pop out. "Houdini. I know you did something. Come out here now so we can make it right."

His pink nose sniffed over the wooden shelf-turned-walkway and his whiskers twitched.

"Show me."

He scooted out of his hole and stood on his hind legs, holding up some rusty old screw.

"Be careful with that. It looks old. You could cut yourself." She figured it was some piece of trash, so she didn't worry about it. "You want to go for a walk to the beach? I could use some fresh air."

Houdini abandoned the part on the shelf and skittered down the platform, but instead of snagging his leash, he went over to the art station Bri had set up for Julie this morning. He nudged a paintbrush with his nose.

"Not you, too." She threw her hands up in the air and headed for the door. "I'll go on my own walk. It's been thirty years. I'm not an artist anymore. Let's move on." She grabbed the old brass doorknob to wrench the swollen wooden door free of the frame, but she never had the chance. It flew open, hitting her in the nose and sending her tumbling back against the display. Postcards, key chains, and other junk scattered across the linoleum floor.

Her head hit the register table, and she was twisted around the wire rack when she settled into her final resting place. She looked up to see two men, smelling of diesel fumes and ocean air, disheveled and wearing stained clothes, shoeless, yet ruggedly handsome with soft eyes and horrified expressions. "If you came to rob me, you won't get much. It's off-season." She untwined herself from the unladylike position straddling the wire display rack.

"No. I mean, I'm so sorry." The man who spoke wrapped his strong hands around her arm and lifted her to stand. He was sunburned like a tourist but was dressed like a dockhand.

25

The first man she'd seen under eighty but above eighteen in months. That did something to a lonely widow. It was like dangling a piece of cake in front of women at a Weight Watchers meeting.

"Are you in life-threatening need of some tourist paraphernalia, or do you just enter stores with brute force?" she asked, ignoring the hum inside her body she felt at his touch.

"No. I-I was chasing...something." He released her and ran a hand through his head full of hair. An attractive trait for any man over forty. Good thing Bri wasn't in the shop, or she'd have them on a date before sundown. An idea Julie wasn't ready for now or ever.

"Chasing something?" She chuckled. "Sorry, no bikini-clad beach groupies in here." With a rub to the back of her sore neck, the one with the ache that hadn't gone away since she started sleeping alone at night, she gathered some postcards from a pile on the floor.

The front man, the one who'd been speaking, dropped to his knees with a thud. "Sorry. Let me help with that. I swear I'm not a Neanderthal who tosses women around." He paused, a look of horror on his face. "Oh no, I've hurt you." He reached for her face, but she retreated from his foreign touch. A swipe of her fingers to her nose revealed some blood, which explained the stranger's wide-eyed expression.

She abandoned the mess and found the mirror behind the registration desk to check her face but discovered only a small cut across her tender nose.

He was at her side, scanning the desk as if to find a fix for his mistake.

"Relax, I won't break." She snagged a tissue from the back shelf and dabbed at the cut. The way he looked at her made her feel uncomfortable yet warm inside. It had been a long time since a man paid her attention, even if it was because he'd slammed a door into her face.

"I am so sorry."

"You said that." She eyed his hand wrapped in a dirty rag with bloodstains. "You appear to need more first aid than I do."

"This?" He lifted his hand as if seeing it for the first time. "No. It's nothing."

"You should clean it at least. That dirty rag increases your risk of infection." She raised her brows at him, waiting for him to explain what he wanted.

"I'm Dustin," the other man said, "and my tongue-tied friend here is Trevor. Don't worry. He's housebroken most of the time."

Julie laughed. "I'm glad to hear it." She eyed Trevor, who was scowling at his friend with that sideways, you're-dead-when-we-get-out-of-here gaze men shoot at each other before they pound on their chests. That's what she imagined they did anyway.

"I'm Julie Boone." She dabbed at her cut again. Seeing that the bleeding had already slowed, she tossed the tissue into the trash and returned to cleaning up the mess.

Trevor was by her side before she picked up the first key chain. "Let me help with that. If anything's broken, I'll fix it."

"Nothing harmed. We're good. Besides, no one's going to be coming in here for about three more weeks."

"Why's that?" Dustin asked, deciding to join them in the clean-up effort.

"Because that's when tourist season starts. Mostly returning families and couples. Well, we hope it will be. Hard to say since this area has taken a hit recently."

"Three weeks. That's not much time." Trevor eyed Dustin.

"Time for what?" she asked, stuffing the key chains into the bottom basket of the display Trevor set upright.

"I'm opening a charter business. I have a catamaran and a speed boat to take guests out on adventures." Trevor's eyes lit up as if he knew exactly what he wanted to do with the rest of his life, something Julie envied. Yet, she didn't like the idea either.

"Oh."

"Oh? What do you mean by oh?" Trevor paused his clean-up effort and looked to her with a tilt of his head.

"Nothing. Just that the idea of touristy things in our little town seems so, I don't know, panhandle-ish."

Trevor scanned her souvenir shop. "You have a problem with tourists?"

"No. I just mean that the charm of Summer Island is that it's different from other beach towns. It's quiet and safe and family-oriented. Not full of noise and parties. We had a company here about a decade ago, but he retired and moved up north to live near his kids. It was a relief to give up the loud-music-playing booze cruises. None of us look forward to that returning."

"Do you have a problem with fun?" Trevor chuckled, but she took it as an insult.

"Fun, no. Obnoxious people who damage property, yes."

Dustin handed her the remaining key chains to put into the basket. "I think Trevor has a different business plan in mind. He came down here to escape the big city life and wants his own peace and quiet."

That sounded better, but for some reason, Trevor accusing her of not being fun irked her. It wasn't as if she cared what this stranger thought of her. A man who opened a business that would draw the wrong sort to their quiet corner of paradise.

Once all the merchandise was returned to its rightful place, Trevor stood staring at her as if he wanted to say something but didn't know how.

"So, what brought you into my store today? In desperate need of souvenirs to pass out on your boat as parting gifts?"

"No." Trevor toed the long crack in the linoleum floor. "Actually…" He let out a long breath and ran that hand through his dark waves again. "You're not going to believe this."

Dustin chuckled but put his knuckles to his lips. "I can't wait to hear this," he mumbled.

"We were chasing something, and it ran in here through that hole in your side door. Don't worry. We can get it for you and put it outside or whatever."

"Chasing something? What kind of something?" she asked, but she was already suspicious.

"A creature, like a mole or rat or weasel."

Julie burst into laughter until her eyes watered.

"I'm serious. I know it sounds crazy, but it ran through these tunnel-like structures outside from our beach all the way up the road and into this building." Trevor scanned the shop and moved to the registration desk, peering down into the cabinets and then standing up and eyeing the wood planks that lined the ceiling.

She stifled her laughter and readied for the trouble Houdini tended to bring with him each time newcomers came into her shop. "I believe you."

He paused his investigation. "You do?"

"I do, but it wasn't a mole or a rat. It was a ferret." She crossed her arms over her chest and faced Houdini's hiding hole that she assumed he retreated to when the men entered her shop. "Houdini, get out here now." She tapped her foot and waited.

"That thing has a name?" Trevor asked with a hint of disgust to his tone that she didn't like.

She sighed and moved the stepladder under the hole to climb up. Trevor wouldn't be the first to take issue with a thieving ferret. "He does. Let me guess... That rusted old screw belongs to you."

"It isn't rusted and old. It's an engine bolt." Trevor sounded indignant.

Dustin clapped his friend on the back. "No, she's got it about right. It's old, rusted, and worthless except to a forty-eight-year-old divorcé who moved to Florida to restart his life."

Julie dared a quick over-the-shoulder glance and caught Trevor's scowl again. If she guessed correctly, Dustin was in for an earful when they left her shop.

Houdini's pink nose and whiskers made an appearance but no more of him before the metal bolt rolled off the platform and into her outstretched hands. "You need to say sorry to these men."

"That varmint's your pet?" Trevor asked with wide eyes.

Houdini popped out, hissed, and ran back into his hole.

"Not nice," Julie scolded.

"Is that thing dangerous?" Dustin asked, backing toward the door as if her two-pound ferret could take down all hundred and eighty or so pounds of him.

"No. He's gentle, kind, and sweet."

"I'm not seeing that," Trevor grumbled.

"Can't make fun of my shark phobia anymore," Dustin said

loud and clear, but she didn't follow. Obviously some inside joke between them.

Julie made kissing noises, trying to get Houdini to come back out. "He's upset that you called him vermin, that's all. He really is a sweet thing. Poor little guy was abandoned by some tourists who brought him here, and the town has looked after him ever sense."

"I'm sensing a trend in your dislike of tourists," Trevor stated, as if it were a fact, not an opinion.

"Dislike, no? Distrust—only the loud, obnoxious, left-my-brain-at-home kind." Julie avoided any further discussion about the type of person who vandalized her store the week after Joe died because they were upset she didn't open the shop that day. "Houdini's really smart. He brings Mr. Mannie his morning paper, he checks on Mrs. Watermore each day and helps get things off of out-of-reach places, and he keeps me company. However, I'm afraid that with intelligence comes a certain amount of mischievousness."

"If you say so," Dustin said in a you're-an-eccentric-ferret-lady tone.

She'd show them how wrong they were about her sweet boy. "Houdini, come out now or you'll be kept in the house for a week. No tunnel time or visits to your friends."

Houdini nudged to the edge of the shelf, stood on his hind legs, put his paws together, and bowed his head.

"That's a good boy. Now, you're staying inside the rest of today." Julie went to the side door and pushed the hatch lock over into the eye, sealing the tunnels from Houdini.

He whined, tugging at her heart. She'd play with him this afternoon and snuggle with him while she worked so he wouldn't be too disappointed.

She handed Trevor his old rusted bolt that he'd made

such a fuss over. Before she could usher them out of the shop, the front door swung open and in strutted a smiling, meddling, blast from the past, Wendy "Wind" Lively. "Good afternoon," she said in her flirtatious, fun, everyone-will-notice-me way. "Who do we have here?" She touched Trevor's arm as if to analyze his strength, and the way her gaze moved from his head to his toes made Julie want to slap instead of hug her long-lost, reappearing friend. "Not bad. Based on my conversation with your daughter, I thought you were hard up and lonely. Guess she had it wrong. Jewels has got game."

Julie flinched at her words. A heat crept up her neck, and she wondered if it was a summer moment or embarrassment. These days it was hard to tell. *Jewels.* A name she hadn't been called for a long time. It didn't fit her anymore. She was no longer the creative, unfocused child who drew pictures on friendship beach or created art out of street lamps and honeycombs.

Wind strutted over and plopped her purse on the registration desk.

"I haven't seen you in over thirty years, yet you waltz into my life again in the same old embarrassing way as if a day hasn't gone by."

"I know, I look great, don't I?" She tossed her long hair behind her shoulders and gawked at the men. "I'm glad you're moving on, but I think you should start off dating just one for now. Until you get your dating legs back anyway."

Trevor moved away from Wind, which made Julie think the man wasn't such a nuisance. "They were just leaving." Julie opened the door, cringing at her rude behavior, but she'd learned years ago that the best way to handle a situation when Wind walked in was to clear the room.

Trevor held up the metal bolt in his hand. "Thanks for getting this back for me."

Wind blocked his exit. "Wait, not so fast." She smiled that millions-of-people-look-at-me smile. "I was only teasing. No need to run away."

"Not running. I just need to return to work before daylight hours are gone." Trevor tilted his head to have Dustin follow him to the door.

Julie cleared her throat. "No problem, and sorry for the inconvenience and for my choice of friends. My only defense is that we were children when we met."

"I understand embarrassing friends." He looked to Dustin, who held his hands up.

"What?" he asked with an innocent smile.

"You both look exhausted and hungry." Wind clapped her hands together. "I know, beach barbeque. We'll bring food, you bring the beverages, and we'll cook at sunset together."

"Did you check the weather?" Julie blurted, as if that would halt the Wind Lively show.

"It'll be fine." She waved off the notion that her plan was flawed, and Julie prayed Trevor and Dustin would make a quick escape before she continued her attention-seeking show.

"Thanks for the offer, but we're really busy." Trevor shot Dustin a sideways back-me-up-here look.

Dustin clapped his hands together once. "Sounds like a great idea."

"Good. 'Cause my friend here needs a fun night out. She's been on her own too long and needs some social time. If she remembers how. Heck, she was married twenty-something years." She cupped the side of her mouth and play whispered, "He's not around anymore, though, so she can have fun again."

Then dropped her hand to her side and announced, "It's settled. Five-thirty at the end of our street."

Trevor opened his mouth, but Dustin shot an arm out in front of him as if protecting a child when slamming on the car brakes. That's what Julie wanted to do: slam the brakes on this conversation.

"We'll see you both at five-thirty." Dustin pressed his palms to Trevor's stomach, which appeared to not even jiggle at the motion, and pushed him out the door.

Julie collapsed onto the step stool, feeling like she'd been in her own wreck. She had been—attacked by a Wind Lively waterspout and had the whiplash to prove it.

Wind threw open her arms, as if waiting for her standing ovation. "You're welcome."

Julie didn't know what to do about the date or about the impending return of her old friends, but she knew one thing —it felt as if her life was finally about to be shaken up. And if she were being totally honest with herself, there was a tiny part of her that wasn't altogether unhappy about that.

CHAPTER FOUR

THE AFTERNOON TURNED TO EVENING, and Trevor had accomplished most of the rebuild. He only hoped it would work when he was done. Dustin hovered around looking at his watch every thirty seconds and grumbling something about being late.

"You go ahead." Trevor waved him off, still analyzing the remaining bolt, not sure why it was left over.

"Not without my wingman."

"You didn't just say that." Trevor rolled the bolt around in his palm, realizing he had little confidence the engine would work. What had he been thinking? He'd come here to make a new life for himself, but all he'd made was a mess.

"You're procrastinating because you've lost your game." Dustin looked at his watch again.

"I didn't lose something I never had." He stood, shoved the extra bolt into his pocket, and stared down at the large metal object sitting on the blanket at his feet.

"Listen, man. You need to find your confidence again. You

used to rule the world of dating. Women still look at you like you're a god, but you don't notice anymore."

Trevor had never lacked confidence. He'd played on the football team in high school, graduated top of his class in college, climbed the corporate ladder to CEO, but something had happened in recent years. He assumed being cheated on would do that to a man. Not a feeling he liked. Determined to put the engine back, he went to assess the tubes and wires that needed to be tucked out of the way. "Have you seen zip ties?"

"No, but nice deflection."

"I haven't noticed any women flocking around me." Trevor headed for the house to escape the invitation and Dustin's constant nudging for Trevor to date.

"Man, you're blind. That Jewels woman fell at your feet."

"That happens when a person is knocked down."

"I meant it metaphorically." Dustin huffed and slammed the glass sliding door behind him.

Inside the house, Trevor didn't find any reprieve, but he didn't want to go to some beach party with women he'd met earlier that day. He wasn't seventeen and hard up. It felt wrong, even after signing the divorce papers. He needed time to adjust to single life again. He needed to be on his own for a while more than anything else. He'd thought since he had waited until he was forty to marry, he'd get it right. Apparently, he'd been mistaken. Just like his own parents who he'd judged for so long, his marriage failed too. The only decision in his life he'd ever regretted was getting married in the first place, but when she said she never wanted kids, it felt like fate for them to be together. No other woman wanted a man who probably couldn't give them a baby. He'd learned that the hard way at a young age. "I'm not going. You go."

Dustin plopped onto the couch like he was back to being his college roommate, begging him to skip studying to go hang out. "Man, I thought you'd snap out of it by now."

Trevor avoided that conversation and picked up his phone to look up engine repair guys near him. He swiped up to find the news app headline: "Business Mogul Rhett Darington Engaged to Lingerie Model Marsha Thompson."

Fire erupted inside Trevor. No. Not already. The final divorce papers were only signed weeks ago. He tapped the image of his ex-wife in the arms of another man and read further. *We find it shocking after Marsha's recent divorce from the once-hailed "most handsome bachelor," Trevor Ashford. Yet, we can't turn our eyes away from the Marsha love life train wreck. Will she crush another man into becoming a hermit, or will Rhett be able to handle this gold-digging beauty?*

"What is it?" Dustin asked, sitting up straight. "I know that look."

Everything inside Trevor screamed that he wanted to punch something or kick something or scream something at the world. It wouldn't help, though. He eyed the picture and felt nothing for the woman with the fake smile and false intentions. That was his past, and he needed to look toward his future. "It's nothing."

Dustin snatched the phone from Trevor's hand. "No, are you serious? That woman is pure evil."

"No, she's not." Trevor knew her better than most, and evil wasn't the problem. For such a beautiful woman, she lacked confidence, and she'd sucked his from him over the seven years they were married.

"You're still defending her? How could you still be in love with that woman?"

Trevor blinked, shaking his head, shedding the eight-year-old fog from his brain. "Love her? No, I don't even like her. But that doesn't mean I don't feel sorry for her. That woman is damaged and will never be happy." He took the bolt from his pants pocket and handed it to Dustin.

"What's this?" Dustin asked.

"You said you'd pay to have my engine fixed. If that's the price you want to pay to go tonight, I'm in."

"Really?" Dustin tossed Trevor's phone down on the table. "Yes. Let's go. Well, after you shower. Dude, you stink."

Trevor looked down at his hermit appearance and made a decision. It wasn't time to hide from the world. It was time to start living again. He wasn't looking for romance, but dinner on the beach sounded easy and fun. How long had it been since he'd had either of those things? "I'll pay you back when I can move some money out of my investment accounts."

"Nope, it's my gift to you. And me." Dustin laughed. "I hate boat work."

"I never would've guessed." Trevor headed up the stairs but paused. "One thing, though. I'm not going to hook up with a woman. I'm going so I can start enjoying life with some friends. Got it?"

"Breaking hearts already?" Dustin lifted his arms over his head and turned to the four corners of the room, announcing, "Ladies and gentleman, our heavyweight heartbreaker is back."

Trevor shook his head and escaped to the small master bathroom. Master was a strong word. It was small and in need of repair, but it was quiet, and it was his.

After his shower, he headed downstairs, determined to have a fun night. The article had said one thing right... He'd been hiding from the world, and it was time to crawl out of his hole. Especially if he wanted his new business venture to take off. Two broken-down boats were only the start. After one season, he hoped to buy more boats out of the proceeds and build up to being the most sought-after charter company on the East Coast.

When he was done getting ready, it was only five o'clock, so they still had time to go to the store to buy some beverages and make it to the beach before sunset. He only hoped this Jewels woman wasn't looking for something serious. He'd keep his distance, but he knew what it was like to be recently divorced, so he'd be kind. Friendship. That's what he wanted from her, nothing more. Sure, she was pretty, in a mothering sort of frumpy way in her shorts and too-big top, but that wasn't enough. He'd learned that the hard way. It didn't matter what she wore. Even in a formfitting dress, with a pretty smile and slim waist, he wouldn't look twice. Not tonight. Not ever again.

JULIE HID AWAY in her room with Houdini at her side. The little rascal always provided the comfort she needed and had been a blessing since Joe died. Why did everyone think she needed to get out of the house and socialize, to start dating, to move on with her life? What was wrong with the way she was living?

She stroked Houdini's soft fur and relaxed to the sound of his snoring. With eyes closed, she took a moment for herself after dealing with Wind all afternoon. That woman was something. Had she always been that vivacious? Yes. Memories flooded in of Wind cheering on top of the lunchroom table on game day, or doing backflips down the hallway because it was Friday, or singing between classes as if providing an impromptu concert.

Back then it was fun and exciting. The girl lived for attention her entire life, probably because she never got any at home. How could she with six brothers and sisters? When the four of them were alone on Friendship Beach, though, life was perfect and calm. Perhaps tonight, despite only going to the end of the road and not to Friendship Beach, she'd feel a little of that calm that might provide a temporary light in the darkness she'd felt over the last few years. That heaviness she carried in her chest that ached on occasion even now.

Knock. Knock. Knock.

"Come in." Julie shifted Houdini from her neck and rested him on her belly so she could sit up.

"Hi, Mom. Can I come in, or are you going to throw something at me?"

"You're always welcome, hon. I promise not to throw anything."

Bri peered out the door as if to check to make sure no one followed her and then shut it and crawled up on the bed beside Julie. "Oh my goodness, you told me about Wendy when I was growing up, but to be honest, I thought you exaggerated. That woman is all energy and needy. How are you two friends?"

Julie thought for a moment, but it didn't take long to extract the information from her memory. "I know she is a lot to take in at first." Julie stroked Houdini, who purred his approval. "You know, in the last few hours of chatting with Wind, I can tell you that she focused the conversation on me and my life and shared little of her own. I know she broke up with someone recently but didn't elaborate. She is working on a new show, but I don't know where. She arrived on Summer Island early so she could help her second oldest sibling this week while she recovers from some minor surgery. Which doesn't surprise me at all, because as big of a personality as she has, she has an even bigger heart. That woman would do anything for you without question."

Bri snuggled up into Julie's side to pet Houdini, causing him to stretch and then rolled over with a playful slap and giggle sound she'd learned was called dooking. "Really? I'd think she was too self-absorbed to notice anyone else."

Julie smiled. "Did I ever tell you about when Tom Wallace dumped me the night before the homecoming dance? The four of us—Kat, Trace, Wind, and I—all planned on going together with our dates. He wasn't even going to tell me and planned to leave me at home waiting in my dress the night of the dance, but Kat found out through a friend that he was taking another girl."

"What? That scoundrel." Bri stiffened. "I hope you ran him over with your car."

"I never even had to think about how to handle it because Wind took care of it."

"What did she do?"

Julie laughed. "You mean after she found out and was so mad she took a one-hundred-eighty degree turn and spun out, taking out a stop sign and almost ending up in a neighbor's pool?"

"What?" Bri shot up. "You could've been killed."

"We were young and thought we were indestructible. Anyway, she snuck out of her house that night, took shoe polish, and wrote all over the school windows that Tom Wallace had herpes."

Bri covered her mouth. "Oh my goodness, that's so mean."

She dropped her hands to her lap, as if remembering what he'd done, and said, "Good for her."

"That's Wind—protective, giving, loving, and exhausting all in one conversation." Julie realized something in that moment. "You know, I jumped to the conclusion that Wind wanted to invite those two men out tonight to the beach because she wanted the attention, but that's not the case."

"It's not?" Bri asked.

"No. She did it because she thought that's what I needed. The woman doesn't stop to ask. She makes assumptions and pulls the trigger on the craziest schemes before you know what's going on. That's what I always loved about her. I never knew what would happen next. She kept life interesting."

"Until she was gone and you were left behind." Bri scratched Houdini's head.

"Is that what you think?" Julie realized she'd been struggling with that same assumption for a long time, but it wasn't true. "You know, that night that I was dumped for homecoming and Wind made that crazy gesture, do you know who really came to my rescue?"

"Who?"

"Your dad." Julie felt the warmth bubble up inside her at the memory. "He was a year older and had plenty of girls to choose from, but when he heard what his so-called friend had done, he came to my house and asked if he could have the honor of taking me to the dance."

"He did that?" Bri beamed with pride. "I knew you two went to the dance and were inseparable from that night forward, but you never told me that story."

"Yes, that's what I loved about your father. He was a good and honest man. We had a great life together." Julie stroked her daughter's hair.

"I miss him, too," Bri offered.

Before they fell into the pit of mourning, Julie decided to focus on the positive. "You know, I may have thought about art over the years, but if I had the choice to make again, I wouldn't change my decision. I'm happy here. This is my home. My friends didn't feel the same way, and they had a right to live their lives the way they wanted to, so I let them go."

"Sounds like Wendy isn't the only friend who put others before herself." Bri crawled to the end of the bed, stood up, and held out her hand. "I think you need to go tonight, Mom. If not to meet a new guy, then to spend time with your old friend. She sounds great. A little much, but a good friend to have."

"I think you're right." She set Houdini in his favorite little spot between two pillows, stood, and straightened her button-down shirt.

Bri opened the door, but before she could leave the room, Wind bolted in with a gasp. "No, no, no."

"What?" Julie asked, not sure she really wanted to know the answer.

"You're not wearing that grandma-frock. You're too pretty and far too young to be caught dead in that." Wind opened her closet and rummaged through until she pulled out a sundress. "Here. Wear this."

"On the beach? With the wind?" Julie shook her head. "I'm not in the mood to be arrested for indecent exposure when that skirt flies up, and how am I going to sit on the sand? I'll be extracting grains from unmentionable places for days."

Bri smiled. "I don't know, Mom. I think you'll look nice."

"Great, now you're ganging up on me?"

43

"It's settled. Wear the dress. Bri, get my makeup bag off the dresser in my room."

Julie eyed the sundress she'd bought two years ago but had never worn. "Fine." She took it, knowing they were both right, that hiding in her home the rest of her days wasn't a way to live. But the idea of meeting a strange man on the beach after all these years churned her stomach up into knots.

"Stop that," Wind said bluntly.

"Stop what?" Julie slid on the dress, feeling the silky fabric against her skin.

"Overthinking it. We're going to the beach to roast some hotdogs and watch the stars and surf. To have fun. That's it." Wind cleared her throat and took off in another conversation direction. "Your daughter's cool. Good job on that one."

Julie chuckled at her sideways compliment and eyed herself in the full-length mirror. If she was honest with herself, she did look pretty in the dress. The way the material was cut made her waist look tiny, and it was long enough to hide her slightly loose skin on her thighs.

Wind shoved Julie into a chair, snagging the makeup bag and a hot iron before Bri could step into the room. They attacked as if commencing brain surgery on a dying patient. Memories flooded in of their high school makeover nights, where the four of them would do facials, nails, and hair for one another. They had been the best times of Julie's young life. And she'd missed them more than she'd allowed herself to believe. In a week, she'd be facing all three of them, though. Would it be a blessing like before, or a curse to show her how much she'd missed in life remaining in Summer Island while they had all gone off to live full lives?

Despite everything she had said to Bri, she still worried that in the end, she'd face a different truth. That now that Joe was gone and her friends and daughter had lives, she had nothing in this world left. At forty-nine, she'd lived her life, and that was a depressing thought. One she knew she had to face and change, despite how scary it was. Tonight would be the first step in the right direction. A step toward a new chapter.

She only hoped her book had a second happily ever after.

CHAPTER FIVE

THE SURF POUNDED onto the shore at a steady beat that calmed Trevor's soul. He enjoyed the sounds of nature in this small corner of the Sunshine State. Waking in the morning to the seagulls' song and falling asleep to the beat of the surf had agreed with him.

Trevor dug a ditch beyond the reach of the surge, and Dustin dropped driftwood into it. The night sea air was pleasant and invigorating, making Trevor feel alive and free, like he could take on anything, even a broken-down boat. Well, after Dustin paid to have the motor fixed.

"Don't even think about ditching me to go be alone with your newest crush," Trevor warned.

"Relax, we're just a couple of friends having dinner under the stars. You brought the wine, right?"

"Yes. Beer and soda, too." Trevor shifted the cooler so it would be out of the way.

Once the fire grew to hearty flames, they pulled two old logs onto the beach to sit on and spread out a blanket for the food. He eyed his watch, realizing it was five-thirty-five. He didn't really care if they ditched them, except that he was hungry and didn't want to wait any longer to eat. At least, that's what he told himself. "If they don't show in a few, we could go hit that little place on Main."

"Already trying to run away?" Wind, the vivacious woman with painted lips and nails, trudged onto the beach and straight for Dustin. Trevor thought to warn his friend that he was wrong, sharks could walk on land and one was circling him now, but he kept his thoughts to himself.

Julie, the woman who'd been wearing baggy clothes and a hat earlier, sauntered from the road to his side wearing a sundress that was formfitting on top and flowed from her hips around her legs. The shock at her transformation stole his speech.

She stopped a few paces from him and held up a box. "Food?"

"Right. Sorry. I, um, didn't recognize you." Trevor stumbled over his words and the log, nearly face planting into the fire.

"Smooth," Dustin said under his breath.

Trevor shook off his surprise at the frumpy woman turned beach goddess in a matter of hours and focused on the food. He rummaged through, expecting frou-frou afternoon tea–style sandwiches and scones but found hotdogs and chips. Before he even opened up the package of hotdogs, Dustin was off for a walk with Wind, leaving him alone with Julie. No surprise there.

Before he had a chance to settle into awkward silence, she knelt on the blanket and pulled the skewers from the box. "We can get them ready for when they return. Don't worry, she's harmless. Promise. She won't be too much for your friend

Dustin. The girl's all show with no pause button, but she's harmless."

"Too much for Dustin? Ha. More like the other way around." He shoved a hot dog onto the skewer and held it over the fire. "I'm starved. Dustin can make his own when he gets back."

She followed his lead and slid a hotdog of her own onto a skewer and held it over the fire. "Now that you mention it, I'm famished. Wind is on her own, too."

"You're not worried about her walking the beach with a strange man?" Trevor studied the flames licking at the sides of his dinner, plumping it up. His mouth watered at the aroma of hearty meat over an open flame.

"Nope. She's excellent with the mace that's probably tucked in her bra. Trust me. That's a fact little Mikey Moltan will never forget."

Trevor turned the skewer over to cook the other side. "He attacked your friend?" If there was one thing in the world he couldn't tolerate, it was aggression against women. Something his three older sisters pounded into him at an early age.

"No. Never had the chance." Julie laughed, a light, sweet sound that carried away on the breeze. Nothing like the way Marsha used to cackle for attention. "Poor Mikey. He invited her over for a party, but she didn't want to go alone, so I went with her. We got to the house, and it was only him and another friend. Mikey said there were more people out back so she should follow him while I spoke to his friend. I knew the guy from my math class, so we chatted, but within a minute or so she ran back into the room, rubbing her eyes. Mikey hollered and howled like a wounded puppy running around the room. They both coughed and sniffled and cried out. Apparently, when they had reached the back door, Wind could see that there was no one else outside, so she pulled out the pepper spray to tell him what would happen if he tried to put the moves on her, and it accidentally went off."

"That's awful. I can say that I've never been pepper-sprayed, but I can imagine it's uncomfortable."

"It is. Even from the other room, my eyes watered. So you better warn your friend not to put the moves on her."

He smiled, relaxing into their mutual understanding of their friends. "Nah, I'll let him figure that one out on his own. He deserves a good pepper spray. Women are always throwing themselves at him, and he thinks he's something special. All I ask is that you make sure she sprays him where I have a front-row seat. Well, maybe a fourth row. I don't want to be that close to the action."

"Sorry, you probably won't get a chance to see it before the police swoop in. See that house there?" She pointed to a cottage to their right. "I guarantee Old Mr. Mannie is at the window with his binoculars and the telephone by his side with the police on speed dial."

"Small-town life, I guess." Trevor eyed the fading light and wished he could see the sunset, but that was on the West Coast. It didn't matter. He would get up for sunrise tomorrow. It was his favorite time of day.

"Yep, we heard about you two on the SISB line within ten minutes of your arrival."

They settled against the log, side-by-side but with a good distance between them.

"SISB line?"

"Summer Island Salty Breeze line."

"Oh, gotcha."

Despite wearing a pretty dress, she didn't fuss over sitting in the sand or her hair being messed up by the elements. He rested his skewer on the box and tugged the cooler over. "Chardonnay? We weren't sure what we were eating and what you ladies liked, so I have some beer and a bottle of wine and some soda."

"I'm thinking beer with the dogs." She took his hotdog, put it on a bun for him, and then set it down on the side of the box to fix her own. He couldn't believe the woman was actually going to eat something processed and drink beer out of a can while sitting on sand. He wasn't in the big city with a model on his arm anymore. And God help him, he liked it.

He opened a beer and handed it to her. "You're different than I expected."

She took a sip of beer and twisted the bottom into the sand so it stayed upright. "You thought I was some desperate single woman looking for a man to save her from her horribly lonely life?"

"No. Okay, maybe a little. But in all fairness, I only met you hours ago. And that was because your trained pet ferret stole an engine part to get me to your shop." He smiled to show he meant it as friendly humor, but based on her pressed lips and averted gaze, he assumed he looked more like the Joker than Mr. Rogers.

She squirted ketchup down her hotdog. She didn't look upset or offended, but there was something in her expression he couldn't decipher. "You're safe. I'm not interested. This is all Wind's doing."

He didn't like the way her rejection bothered him. Was it a defense mechanism? Dustin would tell him she was playing hard to get, but he didn't think that was the case.

Dustin and Wind headed back their way but then continued past, walking in the other direction. Stars began to twinkle in the fading light. A romantic scene for a nonromantic outing. "Can we start again? I mean, without the ferret and awkward pushing together and abandonment of our friends?"

"Sure." She wiped her hands on a paper towel that had been lodged under the food in the box and offered her hand. "Hi, I'm Julie Boone."

He took her hand. It was soft but strong. "I'm Trevor Ashford. Nice to meet you."

"Nice to meet you. What brings you to our quiet little town of Summer Island?"

"I'm here to start over. Call it a midlife crisis or post-divorce-finding-myself mission, but I quit my corporate job, left all my material possessions with my ex, split half our assets since I wasn't smart enough to require a prenup, and escaped the big city noise for the soft sounds of nature." He'd blurted out his entire situation in seconds. What the heck? He didn't even like talking to Dustin about it. He felt like such a girl dumping on her bestie. It was for the best, though. Now she knew his sordid past that left him broken and not the right sort to find a relationship of more than friends.

He took a breath and readied for the onslaught of questions about his former life.

She didn't ask him anything, though. Instead, she watched the couple walking side-by-side toward them once again. "How long do you think until they hook up then break up?"

He blinked at her, watching her expression to make sure she'd heard his confession. He'd never met a woman who didn't want to talk about it or interrogate him about his state of mind and feelings. He shivered at the thought and decided to embrace her lack of interest as a good thing. "Don't know, but I'm thinking Dustin and Wind are perfect for each other for a few days, which works for me since I need him to stick around a little longer to help get my business up and running. Too much work for one person. Don't get me wrong. I've worked hard before as a chief executive officer, but this is the first company where I'll get to be hands-on instead of in meetings and glued to my computer all the time. If I'm being honest, I'm excited about this new venture."

"I see," she said in a tone that suggested she lacked confidence in him.

"I'm going to make this work. I'll start off small, but then I'll work up to several boats and be running a real charter business by next year."

"That's great."

He didn't know Julie well, but that was doubtful sounding in any tone. "But?"

She shrugged. "Maybe it's not the right business for Summer Island."

"Why do you say that?" he asked, worried he didn't know something about the area.

She shrugged and took a bite from her hot dog as if to stall long enough to think of an answer.

He waited, giving her time to chew and then take a sip of her beverage. "Summer Island is a quiet, family-style town. Tourism isn't booming. It's more for quiet types and repeat customers year after year. Maybe you should go to Cocoa Beach or Merritt Island or Daytona."

"Not an option. I bought this property for a steal. I couldn't afford what I purchased in those areas. Not on the beach, and not with enough left over to remain afloat for a year while I build. Don't get me wrong, I'm not destitute, it's just that what money I didn't spend on the divorce is tied up in long-term investments and I'd pay heavy penalties to access the money." He eyed his hot dog, thinking about shoving it into his mouth to stop himself from being so honest with this woman. "Actually, I was in such a hurry to get away from my former life, I left my house and all that was in it to Marsha, my ex, and got out of town."

"How long were you married?" she asked, her attention shifting from her food to him.

"Seven years."

"Kids?"

"No." He heard the relief in his tone and felt led to say something other than the fact he most likely couldn't have children. That was too personal. "Not that I didn't want them. I'm just glad I'm not putting them through a divorce and all the drama that goes with it."

"I can understand that." She opened the bag of chips and offered him one. "Do you miss her? I mean, are you still struggling with the separation? It sounds recent."

Ah, he'd known it was coming. She just took longer than other women to begin the inquisition of his emotional availability. "No." He chuckled and took a handful of chips, then eyed the ocean. Darkness spread across the sky. "You? Do you miss…"

"Joe. Yes. Not as much as three years ago, but I still do." She took a few chips from the bag and nibbled on them. "Tell me, how big do you want to grow your company? Three or four boats?"

"In the beginning, but I hope to have a fleet by the time I'm done. I'll run the biggest charter business in Florida."

"In Summer Island?" She shook her head. "I told you that this is a small coastal town where families come. You won't get that much business."

"I plan on bringing business to this sleepy paradise. You know, mix things up a little bit."

She stiffened, and her hand hung in the air with a chip near her lips, but she didn't eat it. "Maybe we don't want things mixed up around here. The residents might like it the way it is, the way it's been for years."

"Change can be a good thing." He watched her squirm at his comment. This woman didn't want anything to change. Perhaps after her divorce, she didn't want to move on the way he had. "You've been through too much change already. Is that it?" Trevor understood that. He'd gone from big city to little town, married to divorced, big business to little dump all in a matter of months. But he would never let life pass him by without a fight.

"When it's good change, I'm happy to accept it. I'm not sure that bringing in a bunch of spring breakers from high schools and colleges is a good change. Summer Island is all about community, family, and that special small beach town feel. I don't want it to go commercial."

"You own a souvenir shop. You should want more business."

"It's complicated." She turned her attention to the beer at her side as if contemplating where the invention of a can came from.

"If you say so, but maybe if you gave it a chance you'd find that the extra business would be a good thing. You should want customers year-round instead of seasonally."

"Now you sound like a man telling me how to run my business." She shifted, an air of agitation showing in the way her lips tightened. It reminded him of Marsha before she lit into him about how he should be more giving like his secretary.

"Don't compare me to your ex-husband. Not all men are

the same, you know. You divorced, and now you need to move on."

"Deceased."

"What?" he asked, feeling shame seeping in around him.

"Deceased. My husband is dead. I'm not divorced. I'm a widow."

CHAPTER SIX

THE MORNING SUN wasn't up yet, but after a night of tossing and turning, Julie couldn't remain in bed any longer. She slipped out of bed, leaving Houdini to stretch himself awake, and then tip-toed downstairs and made some coffee, careful not to wake her daughter or Wind. Last night's interrogation about what happened with Trevor and why things seemed tense when Wind and Dustin returned to the fire had been bad enough. She didn't need a repeat before her caffeine fix. She was second-guessing her invitation to Wind to crash at her place last night before Wind headed to her sister's.

The rich aroma of her special Jamaican Blue Mountain blend she had saved for the mornings she needed an extra pick-me-up filled the kitchen with the promise of a brighter day. The last gurgles announced the end of brewing, so she doctored it with only a splash of cream and headed to the back porch to enjoy some peace.

Seagulls sang and swooped around on the nearby shore, feasting. Julie took a sip and savored the rich, fresh-roasted taste and closed her eyes. Tranquility. That was Summer

Island. The thought of tourists invading from all areas of the world, causing noise pollution and trash and graffiti, chipped away at her peace.

The glass sliding door behind her opened, so Julie braced for Wind to blow away her morning peace. "Is this section reserved for moping and complaining, or can anyone join?" Her daughter's voice soothed her mood, but her words irked her.

"It's a free porch. Anyone is welcome."

"Even Wind?"

"There might be certain hours reserved for quiet time." Julie sipped her coffee once more, savoring the calmness the warmth brought with each swallow. "But I'm not in a mood."

"Really?" Bri paused. "Houdini, you stay inside." The glass sliding door closed, and Bri sat by her side with her own mug in hand. "It's Jamaican Blue Mountain. I know what that means." She took a sip and then held the mug between her hands and looked out between the buildings toward the distorted beach view between the other homes and shops. "Don't worry about it. If you didn't like the guy, it's no big deal. The point was to get you out of the house."

"I don't dislike Trevor. He's nice enough."

"Nice enough, huh?" Bri shifted to face Julie. "What happened last night? Did he make you feel uncomfortable?"

"No. He was a perfect gentleman."

Bri relaxed back into her seat. "Is he obnoxious, rude, self-absorbed?"

"No."

"Well, you can't deny he's handsome."

She shrugged and hid her expression behind her mug. Her daughter would know with one glance that Julie couldn't deny the man could stir up feelings she'd hoped were long dead inside. Especially for another man besides her husband.

"Then what is it? You feel like you're cheating on Dad? 'Cause Mom, you shouldn't feel that way. Dad wouldn't want you to stay hidden in this place away from the world."

"I'm not hiding. Why does everyone think I don't want anything to change? It's not that." Her hackles rose, but she didn't like getting short with her daughter, so she forced a calmness she didn't feel about life.

"Ah, I see." Bri sounded smug, all-knowing.

"See what?"

"Trevor is offering change. Change is something Julie Boone has never done well with in her life."

"I don't mind change."

Bri pointed to the studio-turned-storage-unit. "That's why you still have every tool, gadget, and memory shoved in there, unable to let it go?"

Julie didn't like where the conversation was going. "What about you?"

Bri shifted like the chair was as uncomfortable as the question. "We're talking about you right now."

"Enough about me. I've lived my life. What about you? Did you quit your job and come home out of some misguided obligation that you need to take care of your mother in her dotage?" Julie spun around and withdrew from her daughter, far enough away so her aging eyes could focus on her. "I'm fine, so you can return to your life now."

"I don't want to."

In that moment, Julie knew one thing. She needed to prove to her daughter that she was good and didn't need her to stick around. The one change she wouldn't tolerate in life was her daughter giving up her future to stay at home because she was worried about Julie. "You're not staying here. I've moved on with my life, so should you."

Bri let out a long sigh. "Don't worry. I'm set financially. I just wanted a break. I'm considering my options and what I want to do next with my life."

Julie thought about arguing that she needed to get back to work, but Bri was many things, and lazy wasn't one of them. And as far as her finances? The girl had been managing her own since she scored her first babysitting job at thirteen. Responsibility was something she'd inherited from her father. "If you need a break, fine. But then you go return to your life after my birthday."

"We'll talk about that later. Nice changing the subject, though. Listen, I get why you had a bad evening and you hate the guy, but maybe you should give him a chance."

"It wasn't a bad evening, and I don't hate the guy." Julie lowered her cup to her lap. "He doesn't want to change *something*. He wants to change *everything*. Did you know he plans on turning Summer Island into a cliché? A tourist trap where the charm of this town is replaced by billboards and chain stores?"

"He said that he wanted to put up a billboard? That's against town ordnance." Bri arched a brow, as if to challenge her mother on the facts.

"No. That's just an example."

"Okay, so what exactly does he want to do to the town that has you so upset?"

Julie eyed that darn storage unit and knew it had been long enough and she should empty it. She should let go of things that didn't mean anything except to clutter up the studio she once dreamed of using. How could she, though? To clean it out was to officially say goodbye to her old life and accept she had to live again. Was she ready to do that? She took a few gulps of coffee, buying herself some time to think of an acceptable answer, but in fact, she didn't know what his plan was. None of it. "Specifics don't matter. He wants to bring in tourists. That's enough."

"So you condemned his plan without even knowing how or what he was going to change? Hmm, sounds like you really have a great reason to snub the guy."

"I'm not snubbing him," Julie said. "I saw him last night, remember?"

"Yes, but you're hiding on this porch instead of going for your morning walk."

She studied the world around her. "I didn't feel like walking today."

"Then go for a swim or a paddleboard outing. How long has it been since you paddled across Banana River and out to Friendship Beach?" Bri stood, taking her cup and her meddling with her before Julie could even answer.

The glass sliding door opened again to the sound of Houdini chattering his discontent at being left in the house. Bri gave her an over-the-shoulder move-on-with-your-life look. "I'm just saying, you could use some inspiration instead of hiding away here."

"I'm not hiding." Julie snipped, but the door shut before her words could reach Bri. Not that she would've listened anyway. Her daughter was right, though. As much as she hated to admit it, Julie hadn't been living, not really. And she had condemned Trevor's idea without even listening to his plan, if he even had one. The guy had been through a lot with his divorce. That was obvious, based on their conversation last night. It wasn't her place to pry, so she hadn't asked any questions about what happened, but she gleaned it wasn't pretty, whatever it was. It wouldn't have hurt her to be friendly, neighborly.

That was it. If he understood what the town was all about, he wouldn't want to bring in strangers and big business. He'd fall in love with the way it was now and not want to change it. And if she spent more time with Trevor, Bri would see she'd moved on and return to her own life. Julie entered the house and spotted Bri at the refrigerator. "Change of plan. I'm taking that walk after all."

There was no *I told you so* or *it's about time*, not from Bri anyway. But when Julie spotted the big red circle on the calendar around the number fifty she paused. Avoidance wasn't going to work for her anymore. "And this afternoon, if you're not busy, why don't we go through your father's old things and donate what we don't want."

Bri wrapped her arms around Julie's middle and rested her head on Julie's shoulder. "I'd like that. Dad would love the idea of donating his tools and possessions to someone in need. There's the shelter in Cocoa Beach… We could ride out there tomorrow and deliver the stuff if we get done tonight."

"Thanks. I'll be fine. Unlike what everyone thinks, I'm strong enough to handle life without your father. And as for change? I might not love it, but that doesn't mean I'll hide away here from it."

Wind sauntered down the hall, stretching her arms over her head and squealing loud enough for people to hear three doors down. "Why, is our little Julie Boone finally growing up and ready to spread her wings? It only took fifty years."

CHAPTER SEVEN

THE ENGINE PURRED like a lion with a head cold. Sure it sounded rough, but it was a classic and still had years left in it. And best of all, Trevor had fixed it himself.

"Can't believe you did it, man." Dustin came from the house, where he'd been sleeping the morning away, and eyed the contraption Trevor had rigged to test the engine with the hose and bucket. It would've been easier to hold things in place with some zip ties. Tomorrow he'd head to the store to get some. "Ah, should there be water coming out of it like that?"

"Yes, that's a good thing," Trevor shouted over the noise before he turned off the motor.

"We should celebrate." Dustin pulled his phone from his pocket.

"Hold up, Romeo." Trevor unhooked the hoses and pointed to the boat. "We need to get her back on board."

"Can't we do that later? Wind and I thought it might be fun to go to the beach. There's some sort of special place only locals know about. It's called Friendship Beach."

"You do know that is only accessible via watercraft, right?"

"Watercraft?" Dustin slid his phone back in his pocket. "Like you have to get to it by boat?"

"Or paddleboard, kayak, or swim."

"Swim? In the ocean?" Dustin shook his head and must've decided manual labor was the lesser of the two evils rather than facing his irrational fear of the ocean and sharks.

Trevor grabbed one side of the blanket while Dustin grabbed the other, and they slid the motor back to the ropes and pullies he'd rigged to get the engine out. His cut looked a little irritated but better than yesterday, so he'd go in and clean and disinfect it once they had the engine back in the catamaran.

It took longer to maneuver it back into the engine bay than it had to remove it, but they managed the job after a few curses and a few more cuts and bruises. "I must be a really good friend to stick around and help with this. You should appreciate me more."

"Don't lie. You're here for the sun and women." Trevor managed to reconnect everything and then decided he should get cleaned up and attend to the cut, which had turned red, on his hand.

"Speaking of women, before I hop on a concall, I'm going to text Wind and see what's going on today. Maybe we can find some trouble somewhere."

"I'll get cleaned up and make some brunch. I'm starved." Trevor stripped off his dirty shirt and wiped his face and neck free of sweat.

"You do that. You're starting to look like a beach bum." Dustin went inside, and Trevor followed.

He went up to his tiny, rabbit hole sized bathroom and retrieved his towel and overnight travel kit he hadn't unpacked since arriving in Summer Island. Well, except for his toothbrush and paste. With a lightness he hadn't felt in a long time, he headed back outside.

The best part of the outdoor shower as opposed to his one upstairs was that it would allow someone bigger than a model-thin hobbit to wash themselves. And there was one good thing about living without any real crowds. You didn't have to worry about indecent exposure. No one would be around to see anything.

He turned the lever to full blast and stripped off the rest of his clothes. The refreshing fresh water was warm but not hot. The pressure was better than inside, and it beat against his sore muscles. This was the life. Standing naked near the ocean without a care in the world. Sure, he was flying high on his sense of accomplishment, but there was something about the peace and quiet...

With his eyes closed, he relaxed into a state he could only describe as peaceful. He could've stayed there all day, but his stomach growled, reminding him he hadn't eaten anything but one hot dog and a few chips last night.

Last night... That had been a boat wreck on a jagged coral reef. How could he have been such an idiot? Julie wasn't struggling with being alone because she had divorced some-one. She was a widow. He'd been a fool and knew if his sisters were here, they would've clobbered him over his head with a curling iron.

He finished shampooing his hair, bathing, and shaving, but the entire time he thought about the beautiful, wounded woman who needed a hug, not a cross word or judgment. Of course, that's what got him in trouble last time he'd noticed a woman. He'd fallen for the wounded girl who needed someone to take care of her. That was a dangerous job he wanted nothing to do with in the future.

That being said, he wasn't going to hold back his business plan until she became comfortable with his goals. The woman hadn't even listened to his ideas before she'd packed up and headed home the minute Wind and Dustin had finished eating.

He flipped off the water and snagged his towel. Still in deep thought about Julie and her issues, he stepped out while drying his grown-out, shaggy hair.

"Oh my! Sorry!"

Trevor dropped his towel at the screech of Julie's voice. The woman stood there staring at him in all his bare glory. Her gaze traveled from his head to his toes before she squealed and turned, covering her eyes.

He snatched the towel from the ground and wrapped it around his waist.

"I'm so sorry. I, ah, didn't mean to see you. I mean, I came to see you but not to *see* you." She retreated while stammering on about seeing him.

"Wait. It's fine." Trevor felt the heat rising up his chest, and he didn't think it was from the sun this time.

"I know. I didn't expect you to be naked." She kept her hands over her eyes as if to shield herself from his exposure. "What are you doing out here with no clothes on?" She twisted at her middle to half face him and peered through two fingers. She must've decided him in a towel was decent enough to face, since she dropped her hands to her side.

"I was taking a shower."

Julie huffed. "I get that, but why're you showering outside?"

"Why not? It's nice out here, and I was dirty from working

on an engine. Not to mention my bathroom's too small up there."

"Are you saying you're going to make this a common occurrence?"

"Why not?" he asked, not sure why it was a problem except that she walked onto his land without announcing herself.

"Because you're exposed to anyone who might see you."

He shrugged and stepped toward her. But she shuffled back a step, her gaze stuttering on his bare chest. She blushed. When was the last time he saw a woman blush? Most of the ones he'd met were the aggressors. "Small town, remember? Only crazy ferret ladies might see me," he teased, but held his breath, hoping she didn't mind the humor.

She laughed, so he figured he was in the clear. "Touché. That's what I was here to talk to you about."

"About being naked?"

"No!" She waved her hand in front of her as if to distract herself enough to pull her gaze away from his body. "I mean stop saying that."

"It's true." He nudged closer. This time she didn't back away.

"I actually came for two reasons. Have you seen Houdini? It appears as if he's managed to sneak out somehow again. He was mad that I drank my coffee outside this morning instead of inside with him."

"No, I haven't. Sorry." He was half sorry. That creature could steal something else if he came around. "And the second?"

"Oh, right. I'm here to talk about your plans for bringing in tourism to Summer Island. You were right, I don't love change, but it's for good reason. When you're dressed, maybe we can talk and figure out a way to get some new tourism here that isn't destructive to the town."

"I can talk now."

She shook her head. "No, not here. Not with you standing there…" She waved her hand up and down in front of him.

"Naked?"

That blush reappeared, and it dusted her high cheekbones. "Go get dressed, and then we can talk. I'm not a fancy businessperson like you, but I believe clothes are usually expected at meetings."

"Is that what you want from me? A business meeting?" he asked, toying with her a little to try to see more of that blush.

"Yes. What else would it be?" Julie asked, her chest moving up and down a little quicker than before, and he knew he was getting to her. And she was adorable when she was flustered.

"Okay, I respect your boundaries, and we both decided that we weren't interested in each other, so you don't have anything to worry about. Friends, right?"

"Friends?" The way her voice dipped made it sound like she was disappointed, but she straightened and nodded. "Right, friends who need to meet."

"Then if it isn't all business, can we at least have a brunch meeting? I was just about to cook for Dustin and me."

"It depends."

"On what?" he asked.

"Are you going to be wearing clothes?"

CHAPTER EIGHT

JULIE SAT at the wooden table with two boxes for chairs, fanning herself. It was definitely a bachelor pad. The air conditioning was blowing from a wall unit, but that didn't soothe her possible summer moment. Her mother hadn't gone through the change until she was in her sixties. Certainly at forty-nine, Julie wasn't really facing that now. The hot flash felt different than some of the others she'd had. The ones where she stood at her freezer with the door open, feeling like someone lit a match of kindling inside her body and doused it with kerosine and it only escaped through her pores.

After a few minutes, the heat subsided. Julie could hear Trevor upstairs, and Dustin had to be in another room around the corner on some sort of call since she heard multiple voices, but she thought it sounded like they were coming from a computer.

The aircon cut on again, and she managed to cool off and peer out the window to make sure Houdini wasn't scurrying about. Hopefully he'd gone to Mannie's place, which was most likely what had happened. That's what he usually did when he was pitching a fit from lack of attention. She should've checked there first, but for some reason she figured Houdini might come back for a second round of rusty treasures.

She watched the waves crest in the ocean. There were probably fifteen-knot winds out today. Great sailing weather if Trevor managed to get his boat running. If he didn't, then that would end his desire to start a big destination site. Her emotions were conflicted between wanting to see him succeed and wanting him to fail at the same time.

Trevor passed by, this time in a T-shirt and shorts. Heat surged through her, and she realized it wasn't a hot flash but a hot *guy* flash. She forced her hand not to fan at her face, but the image of him standing with nothing on awoke something in her she thought was grown over with cobwebs and Bengay. Okay, she'd only used Bengay once, after she had hurt her neck.

"Eggs, toast, fruit, pancakes?" Trevor retrieved a skillet. "I know how to make an egg-white scramble if you prefer."

"Waste the yolk?" She blinked at him. "I mean, that's fine if that's the way you prefer them."

"Me? No. I just thought... Never mind." He placed the pan on the stove and took some eggs from the refrigerator.

"Stop thinking all women are the same." She decided it was safe enough now that he was wearing clothing that she could be within six feet of him, so she went into the kitchen. "She did a number on you, didn't she?"

He cracked some eggs into a bowl and used a small fork to beat them into submission, but she guessed he was taking out his regrets on those poor yolks. "Listen, I owe you an apology."

"For what? " she asked. "Wanting to turn my town into a

tourist trap? Scaring Houdini? Strutting around naked in front of me?"

"Hey, that wasn't my fault. It's my property, lady." He played it off, but she could tell he was embarrassed by the way he looked away and kept stirring the eggs way after they'd submitted to any cooking he had planned for them. He finally poured some milk into the bowl, stirred a few more times, and then dropped a bit of butter into the pan with a loud sizzle. "No, for what I said last night about being divorced. I didn't know—well, that, you know."

"What? That I'm a widow?" She said it aloud as if she were sharing a vacation she'd been on instead of an entire life she'd lived with a man. "No need."

"I didn't know." He stopped stirring and turned to look at her. His too-long hair fell over his forehead, and it looked disheveled, out of place, and oh-so-sexy.

"Why would you?" She needed something to do to keep her gaze away from the man by her side, so she rummaged through the cabinets, but he took her hand to tug her to stand and face him.

"Seriously. I never meant to belittle your grief. I tend to tease a lot, and that might be taken the wrong way. Comparing my divorce to your loss is unspeakable of me."

She took in a stuttered breath, attempting to settle into the man's touch. It was only her hand, a friendly gesture, but she'd worried for so long what it would feel like to have another man touch her besides Joe. To her surprise and shame, it didn't feel awkward or wrong. She wasn't sure how to accept the heat radiating up her arm or the way her pulse quickened, but she didn't want to pull away either.

"Forgive me?"

His words pulled her from her distraction and back to

their conversation. "Why do we need to compare grief at all? We each have suffered in our own ways. We shouldn't compare what we've lost, just be there for each other." She swallowed hard. Her mind spun with possibilities with a man for the first time since she was a teenager. It was dizzying. "As friends, I mean."

"I'd like that." The butter popped, thankfully drawing Trevor's attention back to the pan long enough that she could escape his touch and her thoughts.

"I'll get the toast going." She opened three cupboards before he pointed his spatula toward the last one near the refrigerator.

"Something smells good out here." Dustin entered but paused at the sight of her. "Well, hello there. Trevor didn't tell me that you were coming by for brunch."

He snagged three plates from the overhead cabinet. "Relax, she's here to talk about business."

"Right." Dustin backed out of the kitchen. "No need to save me any. I'm going to run out and snag Wind. She says she's hungry and alone."

"No, you're not going to bolt with a lie." Trevor held out the plate with eggs to Dustin.

"Sounds like something Wind would say," Julie slid two pieces of bread into the toaster before she realized they probably thought that she was trying to be alone with Trevor. She wanted to say something to correct them, but sometimes it was better to just shut her mouth or she'd make the situation worse. Of course it was already worse, because she realized she did want to be alone with Trevor.

"Right." Dustin opened the glass sliding door. "Be back later."

"Tell her to check and make sure Houdini's at Mannie's

place. He should be, but I noticed a break in the wire and fixed it on my way here, which made me worry."

Dustin saluted. "Right, the rodent. Got it."

The toast popped up. "I wouldn't say that in front of Houdini if I were you. He might forgive you once, but if you make him mad enough, you'll be sorry."

"I think I can handle a little thing like Houdini. I'm not afraid of him. I can be just as stubborn."

"Don't say I didn't warn you." Julie slid the bread onto the plates.

Trevor leaned in. "Let Houdini teach him a lesson. Just make sure I'm there to see it."

"I heard that." Dustin closed the glass sliding door.

They were together.

Alone.

He must've seen her expression and decided to retreat to the small table. "No need to pull out the pepper spray. Friends, remember?"

She laughed. "I wasn't the one who did that."

"I know, but you looked like you were about to run before you had your food. We don't want to waste those yolks, do we?"

"No, I'm eating." She dug in and enjoyed Trevor's quiet company. They ate mostly in silence with an occasional glance at each other. It had been a long time since she'd sat down for a meal with a man. If she were being honest with herself, it was nice. Too nice.

She focused on her toast, trying not to look uncomfortable. They were friends. That's what they agreed to, so this was a business meeting. A way to find out what he was up to that could mess with the town. That was all. Nothing more.

Then why did her foot keep tapping along with her heart each time she caught sight of his green eyes and sexy hair? Why did she have a jittery feeling in her belly? And most of all, why didn't she feel guilty for finding another man attractive? A man who wasn't her husband.

CHAPTER NINE

TREVOR ENJOYED the easy banter with Julie. For some reason, the minute he'd heard she had lost her husband instead of divorcing, it made him see her in a different light. It shouldn't have mattered, but it did. Perhaps because their marriage hadn't failed and she hadn't chosen to leave her husband for another man. She'd been a devoted wife for years. Many years, based on having a grown daughter.

Julie pushed her plate away from her and dabbed her mouth with her napkin. "So, you say you want to bring more business into Summer Island."

"It's not only a want, it's a need." He pushed his own plate away from him. "More than anything, I need this business to work."

"Why?" she asked directly, but there wasn't an easy answer.

He thought about it for a moment. "Every business needs customers."

"That wasn't what I asked." Julie smiled and folded her hands. "We're friends, right?"

"Right."

"Why this business? Why here?" Julie asked.

He hesitated. "Honestly?"

She nodded.

"Dustin says it was my midlife/divorce crisis."

"No, why do you think you chose this place? What do you see as success here at this chartering business? Do you want to have a bunch of sailors come through to charter your boat with little sailing experience? Do you want to have spring breakers vomiting all over the decks? Or do you want families to go out and enjoy adventures on the ocean and sandbars?"

He thought about it for a minute and then sat forward, resting his elbows on the table. "When you put it that way, I would say I'd prefer families to have adventures."

Julie smacked her hand on the table. "If that's your mission, then I can help you make that happen. There are regulars who come into town. I'll reach out to them with your website or phone number they can book through. Also, we can attend the next town meeting and pass out flyers or cards with your website link on them."

"You would do all that with me?" he asked, shocked at her offer. "I thought you didn't want this business here." He thought for a minute and dared to reach a little further. "Or me."

She studied her knuckles for a moment and didn't look up when she spoke again. "You're not the problem. As for the business, I'm happy to help, as long as you don't turn Summer Island into some party destination." Her hand shot out, and she looked up with the most stunning silver-blue eyes. "Deal?"

He took her hand, welcoming the way her tiny fingers felt around his large hand. She was soft, dainty, beautiful, but strong and independent. He'd never met a woman with natural beauty, self-confidence, and passion like Julie before. "Deal."

A clap of thunder in the distance warned of a coming storm. She withdrew from his touch. "Tomorrow, we'll go around town and I'll introduce you to everyone. Bring some flyers or cards. If you need a printer, there is one on the corner of Sunset and Main. Tell Barb that Julie sent you, and she'll give you a discount."

He welcomed having an excuse to spend more time with Julie, but he had real work to do. "Thanks for such a kind offer, but I have to finish working on the boats if I'm ever going to get my business off the ground. Is it necessary to go meet people face-to-face, or can I just get their email addresses and send them all the information?"

She smiled, a heart-throbbing, girl-next-store smile. "You're not in Seattle anymore. Business is done differently in a small town. You want your company to thrive in Summer Island, then you want the people here to be involved. Trust me.'"

Another clap of thunder warned he better get to work before the storm reached them, ending his workday early. "Okay, I'll give your suggestion a try."

"Be at my place at eight in the morning. Unless that's too early for a city boy like you."

"I'm up at five." He escorted her to the glass sliding door, not because he wanted her to go but because he wanted to get to work. If he didn't, he wouldn't be able to stay in Summer Island, and for the first time since he'd arrived, he wanted to stay for more reasons than hiding from the media.

"I can get the dishes done since you cooked, so you can get to work before the afternoon storm hits. There'll be a lot more of them once the summer months arrive."

He opened the door. "No. I invited you to brunch, and you're helping me with my business."

"It's no trouble. Honestly, maybe helping you with your business will nudge me in a direction for my own. You were right." She glanced through the glass sliding door, as if to see her future in the distance. "I'm not the type to be running a souvenir shop."

He could see the internal conflict within her. The struggle between her past and her future. It was understandable that she was still trying to figure out her new life without a husband. Especially since he assumed they'd been married young. It made him realize the mess of his life was nothing in comparison to what she had faced. "What do you think you might want to do?"

She looked at him, her gaze intense but inviting. "I was an artist years ago. Some of my work won awards and was even placed in the town museum. Nothing compared to big city, but I might try my hand at that again."

"What kind of art?" he asked, opening the door and walking her out. The warm sun caused him to shield his eyes so he could still see her walking by his side.

"It's not traditional painting or sketching, although I do enjoy sketching. I'm an artist who uses nature. My piece that was placed in the museum years ago was said to be ahead of its time. I worked with a retired bee keeper and designed a mold in the shape of a pesticide can. Bees were becoming more scarce in the area, so I did some research and discovered that the new pesticides they were using were having a direct effect on bees producing honeycombs."

"That's not only art, that's political and profound. How old were you?"

"Sixteen."

"I went to parties and drank too much at that age. It wasn't until I was eighteen that I even thought about the world beyond myself." He looked down at her five-foot-fourish frame and saw a giant heart. "I get it now."

"What?"

"Why you don't want tourists here. It's not just about you wanting to keep things the same. You want to protect and preserve what exists. I can respect that." And he could, which surprised him, since the previous company he worked with bought old buildings and tore them down to build parking garages.

"Perhaps, or it could be both reasons." She eyed the path behind the old fence near the Houdini tunnel. "I better go check on Houdini. Dustin might have found himself in some trouble if he called him a rodent. Houdini is sensitive like that."

"I'll walk you home." He didn't get a chance to take a step before his phone rang.

"You should answer that. I'll be fine."

"It's probably Dustin. You might need me to come with you." He glanced down at the screen to discover it wasn't Dustin.

It was Marsha. The ex-wife who ran out without a word, who cheated on him, took everything she could in the divorce without even facing him or speaking to him. The lawyers had handled everything for her. Now, months later, with the divorce final and him moving on with his life, she decides to speak to him? He stared down at her number as if it wasn't real. "It's my ex," he mumbled, but the shock took hold and he didn't say anything else.

He wanted to tell Julie that he didn't want to talk to his ex. He wanted to tell Julie that if he had a choice, he'd rather spend the day with her. He wanted to tell her she was a special woman who he wanted to get to know better.

But he didn't say any of those things because he couldn't comprehend why Marsha would call him now. And God help him, he stared at that phone even after the ringing had stopped, because as much as he was curious about why she was calling, he was equally dreading finding out.

CHAPTER TEN

"Naked?" Wind squealed. "You go girl."

Julie wasn't in the mood for Wind's antics, not when she was packing up the last twenty-something years of her life. She sat on the ground surrounded by boxes, carefully folding an old flannel shirt Joe used to wear. It had been his favorite.

Bri squeezed her arm. "You're doing the right thing, Mom."

"I know."

"Ignoring me won't make me stop asking. Inquiring old friends want to know all the juicy details." Wind plopped down and threw her arms around Julie. "But Bri's right. You're doing great."

The evening breeze swept through the garden and offered a reprieve from the humidity after the rain. Not to mention the dripping sweat from working in the once-studio-turned-storage-room all day.

"So Mr. Mannie was certain Houdini wasn't there?" Julie asked, eyeing the tunnel at the side of the house.

"Don't worry about Houdini, Mom. He's sulking some-where," Bri reassured her, but Julie couldn't help but worry.

He wouldn't be able to find his way home if he got out of the tunnels.

Wind released Julie. "No way you're changing the subject now." She propped her elbows on her legs and held her head between her hands, staring Julie down. "Come on. Give us more details about naked Trevor, girl."

"Nothing to tell. It was an accident."

"Mom, seriously?" Apparently Bri wasn't going to let this go, either. Why had Julie even mentioned it? Because she'd been so flustered, she needed to tell someone.

"How do you accidentally see a man naked?" Wind asked with an air of sarcasm.

"He was showering." The minute the words were out of her mouth, she knew she'd made a mistake. "Outside. He was bathing outside when I accidentally saw him."

"What did he do? What did *you* do?" Bri asked, abandoning her packing and settling cross-legged facing her.

"I screamed. He covered himself. That's it." Julie grabbed her nearby iced tea and took a sip, trying to keep the warmth bubbling up inside her from surging through her. Funny how it happened each time she thought of seeing Trevor naked.

"Wait until Kat and Trace arrive in a couple days. They're going to love this story." Wind took her phone out of her pocket and started typing.

"I think it can wait until they get here," Julie grumbled, not looking forward to the three of them, plus her daughter, playing matchmaker. How could she sit here packing her husband's clothes while talking about another man? It was wrong.

"I'm not texting them. I'm looking up more on our Trevor Ashford. Dustin said he'd been cheated on by his ex-wife and there was all sorts of publicity around it."

"Poor guy." Bri tucked her legs under her, as if to settle in for a while. "Maybe that's why he decided to come to Summer Island. It's a place to get away from it all."

"I think so." Julie twirled her metal straw around her glass, watching the amber liquid swirl. Trevor had said she'd been the one who had suffered more, but that wasn't true. Heartbreak couldn't be measured. She was glad she'd extended an offer of friendship to him. "I'm helping him by providing an introduction to the town tomorrow. He's agreed to concentrate more on family adventures than spring break crowds, so I thought I'd help."

"What did you have to do to convince him of that?" Wind asked in a sensual tone.

"Please, we barely know each other. I'm just helping a new business out while ensuring we keep the charm of our small town intact."

"Barely know him. I think you know him intimately." Wind gasped. "Oh my goodness, Dustin didn't tell me that Trevor was married to *the* Marsha Thompson."

"Who's that?" Julie asked, even though she wasn't sure she wanted to know.

"Only a world-famous model and social diva." Wind dropped her hands, still holding the phone in her lap. "Wow, this guy must not have a type."

"Thanks. I realize I'm not model material, but I have other good qualities."

Bri rubbed Julie's back and handed her another shirt to fold, as if she had to soothe her each time she touched something of Joe's. This was Bri's father. Julie should be comforting her daughter, not the other way around.

"I'm not talking about the model part. She's a head-tripping, manipulative, crazy woman who uses men to further her career."

"Sounds like he deserves a better woman in his life. Hmmm, I wish I knew someone who would be good for him." Bri stood. "Refill?" She took Julie's glass, but Wind waved her off as if she didn't have time to focus on anything but the juicy gossip on the internet.

"It sounds like she's given him some trouble." Julie struggled between wanting to know more and facing further conversation with Wind. "Dustin didn't say anything else?"

Wind shouldered her gently. "Ah, now she wants the deets."

Deets? What was she? Ten years old? "Don't tell me. It doesn't matter."

"Since you twisted my boa, I'll dish." Wind acted like she threw a scarf around her neck and leaned back. "Soooo, Dustin said that the woman cheated on Trevor with his secretary. A male secretary he'd hired because his ex insisted he not work with a woman. She was apparently the extremely jealous type. Despite her infidelity, Trevor tried to make it work. Something about believing in the institution of marriage and needing to try, unlike his parents."

Considering Wind had divorced twice already, Julie guessed she didn't feel the same way about marriage. Julie didn't want to touch that conversation, though, so she folded two more articles of clothing and moved a little out of Wind's reach to work on some tools. "Doesn't sound like the type of woman he'd go for." Julie dropped a rusty saw into the trash with a clammer. "Not that I know him well enough to attest to that."

Wind laughed. "Oh, I think—"

"Stop. I get it." She threw her arms in the air and spun

around in her best imitation of Wind commanding a stage. "We all know I saw Trevor Ashford naked."

"I guess everyone does now," a deep male voice Julie willed not to be Trevor's echoed through the garden, stilling her movement.

She closed her eyes and mumbled to herself, "Please tell me that isn't him behind me. It wouldn't be. It can't be."

"Oh, it is, dear." Wind approached and tapped her on the shoulder. "I'll give you two some privacy," she said loud enough to make sure everyone in the garden heard.

She spun around, eyes open, feeling like someone had used a torch to heat her skin. "What are you doing here? I thought you were busy. I know I am."

Bri inserted herself between them, holding Houdini up with his wiggling nose. "Mom, he brought Houdini back."

"I found him snuggled up in the boat by the engine. He wasn't too happy when I took him out." Trevor held out his arm, showing scratches across his wrists.

"Houdini. No. You didn't."

"Don't be too hard on him. He didn't mean to. I think he was chasing something in his dreams and I scared him."

"Oh, right. I should've warned you. When Houdini's dreaming, you have to call out for him to wake up and not get too close. Mr. Mannie says he has PTPD."

Trevor's brows rose. "What's that?"

"Post-traumatic pet disorder. Mr. Mannie says his old owners were mean to him and he still suffers in his dreams."

"Well, then don't be too upset with the little guy." Despite his wrist lacerations, he scratched under Houdini's chin.

The ferret blinked at them both and turned his head in that way that tried to look innocent. "Okay, but you need to stay inside until I make sure you can't get out of the tunnels."

"I can help you look tomorrow after you introduce me to the people in town," Trevor offered.

Bri quietly back-stepped out of the garden with two thumbs-up behind Trevor's back. Julie ignored her and tried to keep her focus on Trevor.

"That's awfully nice of you, but I'm sure you're really busy," Julie said, picking up another tool and looking at it from different directions to see the condition of it.

"No busier than you, I see. Doing some spring cleaning?" Trevor asked.

"Something like that. I'm donating this old junk." Julie said it and knew it was true, but why was it so hard to get rid of broken old stuff?

"Really?" Trevor lit up, his gaze scanning the area and stopping on something near her feet. "If you don't mind, can I have some of those zip ties over there?"

She followed his gaze to Joe's old box of extras. Bits and bobs of nothing important, but she couldn't give any of it to Trevor. Giving it to a stranger was one thing, but giving it to a *friend*—a friend who each time he entered the room, her pulse quickened—was wrong. "No. I can't give that to you."

"Right. Sorry. I didn't mean to overstep. I can pick some up tomorrow at the local hardware store. No worries. I'll see you at eight in the morning." Trevor rushed from the garden, leaving Julie to face her guilt. The only problem was that she felt more guilt about telling Trevor no than having him in her home. That only made her feel more guilty. She picked up the zip ties and felt the plastic strips between her fingers as if Joe had been holding it moments ago. "Oh, Joe. I don't know how to do this. Bri's right, you'd want me to move on. But how do I do that without hurting your memory?"

A hand rested on her shoulder, so Julie swiped her eyes,

not wanting Bri to see her cry. Julie needed to be the strong one. She was the mother.

"Oh, Jewels. You could never harm Joe. He adored you from the time we were children." Wind's soft, sincere voice soothed Julie. "It's been three years. You need to let him go."

"But I can't forget him. If I do, then he's really gone." The dull ache that had settled in her chest a year ago expanded and intensified.

Wind turned her around and cupped her cheeks. "He's already gone from this life, but he'll always be in here." She put her palm to Julie's chest. "And if I know Julie Boone, she has enough room in her heart for everyone. Hon, you don't have to forget Joe to feel something for Trevor."

"I don't?" Julie trembled. To face caring for another meant she was really letting go of Joe. The man she'd been meant to grow old with. Her homecoming hero. The man she'd married and had a child with at such a young age. "He was gone before I even said goodbye. It was so sudden. Gone before he hit the floor."

"I know, honey. I know." Wind pulled Julie into her arms and held her up. The way she had when they were teenagers when Julie had found out she was pregnant. She was right then that Joe loved her and would want to marry her, but was she right now? Did Julie really have enough room in her heart for the man of her past and a man for her future?

CHAPTER ELEVEN

TREVOR PAUSED at the edge of the road leading to Julie's shop and house. He'd been up half the night, remembering how she'd reacted to his asking for the zip ties. Apparently she'd wanted to put distance between them. That had to be it. The only explanation he could come up with after tossing and turning all night. The situation had been awkward because of her catching him at the outdoor shower. Yes, that's why she'd been so weird when he'd returned Houdini to her yesterday. Had she thought he did it on purpose? Some sort of ploy to get her into his bed?

He shook his head, hoping that's not what she'd thought. He took a deep breath and decided to keep a comfortable distance from her today. Make sure that she knew he wasn't trying to make her feel uncomfortable. That's what they were, friends, and he needed to remember that. After all, he wasn't looking for a relationship, and she wasn't ready for one. Today, he'd make sure he maintained boundaries and concentrated on all things business. If he was ever going to get the town locals to help spread the word, he was smart enough to know he needed an insider.

At the end of the drive, he straightened his collared shirt and held tight to his small box of cards he'd made last night to distribute to the town. Not that he understood how this would help, but apparently things were done differently in Summer Island.

He knocked on the front door and waited.

"Jewels, your date is here and looking hot as ever!" Wind's voice came through the open front window.

Trevor hoped they would escape Wind quickly. He'd already heard it all from Dustin this morning. He'd put all sorts of crazy thoughts in Trevor's head about asking Julie out on a real date and how Trevor was totally falling for the woman but he wouldn't admit it to himself. Hogwash. All of it. What did his friend know, beyond games and dating a different woman every night?

The door swung open, and Julie stood there in a spaghetti-strapped top—a term he'd learned from his ex—and skirt that showed off her tan swimmer's legs. Her shirt was a deep ocean blue, which made her eyes pop like the morning sun cresting the horizon.

"Ready?" She closed the door behind her, leaned into him, stealing his breath, and whispered, "Don't worry. Wind's leaving to help her sister out. She won't be around much today."

"I hope her sister's okay," he blurted, not sure what else to say.

"Minor surgery, so she'll be fine. So, are you ready?"

"Right. Yes." He held up his box of cards.

"Keep an eye on Houdini for me," she called through the open window. "Okay, we'll hit Cassie's Catch first, then the marine store, Summer Sweets, the corner store, hardware, post office, and nail salon. Sound good?"

"Sure." He side-stepped, allowing her room to walk down the path so they weren't so close together.

"Thanks again for doing this," he said while following her down the narrow walkway to Main.

"No problem. I needed to run some errands anyway." She moved around a pothole closer to him, so he moved away so he didn't crowd her.

At the end of the street, they turned left, landing them in the heart of town. The cute, quaint shops were inviting. A restaurant with a large rope net hung from an awning, looking inviting. The aroma of fried fish and other goodies reminded him he'd skipped breakfast in his haste to make it on time to Julie's place.

They strolled into the main dining area, which was reminiscent of an old pirate ship, with wooden plank walls, sails, and a large helm in the center in front of a repurposed mast pole.

"Hey, Cassie. I've got someone I want you to meet," Julie called out the minute they entered.

Trevor retrieved a card from the box and found a burly man with tattoos up his arm wiping his hands on a dishtowel. "Hello. I'm Trevor Ashford. I started a business at the end of Hammerhead Drive. It's a charter business. I have a sailboat and a motorboat, and I hope to take families out on adventures. Here's my card." He held out the card to the man, who looked to Julie as if to translate.

"Where'd you find this stuffed-crabby outsider?" the burly man asked.

"You think?" Julie laughed and opened her arms to the large man.

Trevor didn't like the way the man, who he assumed was the owner Cassie, picked Julie up off the ground in a too-intimate hug.

Once he placed her on her feet again, he turned to Trevor. "Some advice, son."

Son? He was maybe ten years or so older than Trevor. How patronizing.

"In a small town, you might want to say hello before you spout out your entire business plan. Things run a little less cut-throat 'round here. It's part of our charm." Cassie rubbed Julie's back, making sweat pool on the back of Trevor's neck, or was that the heat from the kitchen? Either way, he didn't like it. "How you doing, girl?"

"Fine. How're you and Sandy?" she asked, not seeming to mind his touch at all.

"Great. Hey, I heard that the gang is coming back to town. You gals used to rule Summer Island."

"That was a lifetime ago." To Trevor's relief, she swatted Cassie away.

"Still, I'd be honored if you gals came here for a meal while you're all in town together. I'll throw a fiftieth party for you."

She was turning fifty? She didn't look a day over thirty-five. It was a relief to know he didn't go after younger women all the time like Dustin had accused him of doing. They continued to chat as Trevor stood there smelling seafood and old wood. He was once a man who commanded board rooms and negotiations. Now he couldn't even navigate a simple conversation.

"Tell you what... If our girl Julie here vouches for you, I'll hand out some of your cards to people here." He took the card from Trevor and tossed it on a long table with the rest of the small-town sales paraphernalia. "I've got to get to work, but look forward to you and the girls coming in for a bite."

"Of course. They'll be here tonight," Julie said.

Trevor realized that come this evening, she would be caught up with all her friends and have no time to hang out with him. If he was honest with himself, he didn't like that thought.

They left the restaurant, and Julie halted at the sidewalk. "Okay, what gives?"

"What do you mean?" Trevor looked to the restaurant behind him, the nail salon with the starfish logo across the street, and then to Julie.

"Seriously? I guess Wind was wrong and you're not into me. That's fine, but you don't have to worry. I won't attack you. You don't have to keep moving away from me or acting like some big-city robot."

"I'm not moving away from you. I'm giving you space." Trevor rubbed his forehead, trying to clear the noise.

"Maybe I don't need that much space." Julie flipped her hair away from her face and sighed. "Listen. I know I was rude yesterday, and I apologize for that."

"You have nothing to apologize for," Trevor offered, but Julie shook her head.

"I do, but let's table the why and the bigger conversation for later. We can talk after we're done here, someplace without a dozen prying eyes on us. For now, try not to look like a scared minnow in a shark tank." She took a few steps and halted again. "And try to smile and greet someone before you shove the cards at them."

"I thought you told me to bring these." Trevor looked down at the box in his hand.

Julie grabbed the box, opened it, shoved a few cards in his

pocket—her touch sending a jolt through him—and then put the box on the crumbling brick half-wall in between the restaurant and the marine store. "There, now you can casually pull the card from your pocket once we get to that part of the conversation."

"What do we do with the rest of them?" He pointed to the abandoned cards that took him three hours to create, proof, and print last night.

She waved it off. "They'll be fine. No one wants to take your cards, trust me." She sashayed ahead of him with a mesmerizing sway of her hips that made him follow her to the next stop.

This was his kind of store. A marine shop with all sorts of gadgets and lines and tools. Before Julie had a chance to introduce the owner, Trevor grabbed a wire cutter, screwdriver, sandpaper, and some zip ties and then pointed to the lines. "I need two hundred feet of that, please."

"Sure, stranger. Welcome to Summer Island." The older woman with sun-worn skin and small eyes but a bright smile jumped into action, measuring the line from the huge spool.

"I'm not a stranger. I shouldn't be anyway. I'm a local now. Name's Trevor Ashford."

"Nice to meet you, Trevor. I'm Leslie, but everyone calls me Skip." The woman shook his hand and then went back to measuring and then cutting the rope. "You a sailor?"

"I am. Actually, I'm opening a charter company here in town. At the spot of the abandoned old hotel."

"That's good news. That hotel needs some work, and it's the only one in our town."

Trevor hesitated, but honesty was the best policy. "Actually, I'm mostly concentrating on the chartering business right now. Maybe later, after I earn enough from this company, I can work on the hotel."

Skip slammed her fist down on the counter. "Then let's get you some business. I know lots of locals who love to sail. Ever think about teaching?"

"No. But it's something for me to consider. Right now, I'm hoping to find some nice spots nearby to take people on picnics, bird watching, sea life spotting, anything fun and adventurous would be great."

"I can help you with that. Oh, and also my daughter. She knows all the great spots."

"I've got that covered." Julie stepped out from an aisle and approached the register.

"Oh, Julie, I hadn't seen you there." She rang up the items on her iPad instead of the old-fashioned register sitting on the counter collecting dust.

"Right. I'm sure you could do that. But if Trevor here needs any additional help, my daughter's available." Skip bagged the smaller items and then rolled and fastened the rope so it was easy to carry. "Got a card?"

Trevor retrieved the square, rough-edged card from his pocket and slapped it onto the counter. "Sure do. I can bring flyers or send you an email or whatever you need if you can help spread the word."

"Love to help. I'll get my daughter, Rhonda, to give you a call soon." Skip studied the card as if it were faux currency.

"Thanks, Skip." Julie ushered him out the door. "Don't answer that phone when it rings from Rhonda."

Julie pursed her lips and eyed the store behind him as if it were full of salty aliens. He pulled his sunglasses from his pocket and put them on to shield his eyes from the bright rays so he could see Julie's expression. It was tense. "Why not?"

"Because you don't want to be Rhonda's next victim. We have crazy even in small towns. She'll want to marry you after one phone call. Trust me."

"Why, Julie Boone, are you jealous?" Trevor teased.

"I'm only trying to warn you. Rhonda isn't the right person for you. She's not a kind person. A few years ago, convinced Trace's dad that the city was going to pay him pennies for his land so they could build a road through to connect the main strip with the ocean. He almost sold the property to Rhonda because she'd convinced him that she didn't want to see him leave Trace with no inheritance."

"What happened?" Trevor asked.

Julie smiled. "The town found out and put a stop to it. There are good people here. I want you to meet them, not fall into some black widow's web, especially after what you've been through."

"What I've been through?" he asked, wondering how much Dustin had told Wind, who'd obviously shared with the rest of the women.

She sighed. "You're divorced. I know it had to be hard. Wind looked you up on the internet and told me that your ex was a difficult woman to deal with."

"I told you, my grief is nothing compared to what you've been through."

Julie stepped closer and took the bag from his hands. "And I told *you*, don't compare our levels of grief. Pain hurts. It doesn't matter if it's a cut to the wrists..." She dropped the bag next to the box of cards and lifted his arms to trace the scratches Houdini had left on his skin. Her touch sent shock waves through him. "...or a gunshot wound to the heart." She put her palm to his chest, stealing the breath from his lungs.

"It all hurts at different times in different ways. You have as much of a right to be lost or confused or upset as I do."

In that moment, he knew Julie was unlike any other woman he'd ever met. "Thank you for that."

"Let's finish up here, and then I want to take you to some-place special where we can talk without all the town watching." She hooked one finger around his hand and tugged him toward the next stop on their Summer Island tour.

Julie was the kindest, most honest, fun, easy to talk to, and beautiful woman he'd ever met. Not to mention, the way one finger dusting his skin made his entire body quake, one smile brightened his day, and the thought of one kiss hooking him didn't scare him. One kiss from Julie wouldn't destroy him but would heal every wound—wrists, heart, and soul.

CHAPTER TWELVE

JULIE WAITED at the end of the road with two paddleboards, nervous about sharing more of herself with Trevor. She didn't like feeling vulnerable. Sure, they kept saying they were friends, but the more time they spent together, the more she was drawn to him. And if she wasn't mistaken, or brainwashed by Wind, then he thought of her as more than a friend too. Yet, they both clung to that term. It was safe and allowed them to spend time together without the pressure of dating.

The afternoon sun was high in the sky, so she tugged her hat down a little to shield her face from the damaging rays. Her long-sleeved water shirt was hot but would protect her shoulders and arms, and she'd slathered on sunscreen to protect her legs.

Trevor strutted up dressed in swim trunks and a T-shirt along with his cap. She worried he'd burn the back of his neck or his chest and arms since she doubted his T-shirt provided any SPF protection. "Hey, you."

"Hey. Glad you came." She shifted between feet, the strap

around her ankle that attached to the board scraping at her skin.

"Why wouldn't I?" Trevor removed his flip flops and tossed them to the side, apparently not worried about anyone taking his stuff anymore. "I've got to see this mystery place."

She decided not to mention the real reason she was worried he wouldn't show. No need to be all serious. They were headed out for a fun outing. To a place she hadn't been to in years. "Okay, first things first. Are you wearing sunscreen?"

He nodded. "Yep, face, arms, and legs. Oh, and tops of feet. This isn't my first rodeo on the ocean. I learned the hard way not to ever go out in the Florida sun without protection. The great sun poisoning incident of 2018 taught me that." He eyed her foot and then wrapped the strap from the other board around his ankle.

She picked up her board and led him down the rocky road, onto the beach, and out into the water until they reached the coral bottom and finally soft white sand and seaweed. "It's not a great place to set off from since it's kind of icky, and it won't be an easy ride in the chop today, but we should be good. Trust me, the effort will be worth it."

"I'm intrigued. Only one problem."

"What's that?"

"I've never been on one of these before." He stood there with a broad smile, eyeing the board as if he was about to mount a bucking whale shark.

"Don't worry. We can sit first. Trust me, anyone can do that. If not, then we're in trouble. After that, we'll try up on our knees, and then we can try standing." She straddled the board and started paddling forward so he could have room to get on his.

He picked up his paddle and lifted one leg over the board. A strong gust of wind came through, sending his board sideways. A wave rushed in. He abandoned the paddle and grabbed on to the edges, attempting to stay upright, but it rolled, dunking him under another wave.

He popped up to the surface, swiped his face of water, and snagged his floating hat. "Not a good sign."

She rowed to his side, retrieved the paddle, and held his board still.

"What did you say? If I can't sit on the board I'm in trouble?" He coughed, put his hat inside out to release the water, and then plopped it back onto his head.

"Don't listen to me. I say a lot of stupid things like you can't have zip ties." She wanted to suck the words back in, but obviously she needed to get them out or they were going to haunt her all day.

He rested his hand on her thigh. "Hey, no worries. We'll both get past our issues. It takes time and practice, right?"

A new light shone inside her, forcing the dark clouds from where they had settled three years ago, and the tension in her shoulders let go. "Right." She savored his touch instead of pulling away because it felt tender, friendly, and safe.

He grabbed both sides of the board, leaving her feeling the cold where his hand was sitting a moment earlier. On the first try, he managed to beat an incoming wave and slide his chest up so he lay flat. After the next wave, he sat up, straddling the board with a broad, I-conquered-it-and-so-can-you kind of smile.

She held out his paddle. "Good job. Almost as good as you did talking to all the people in town. If I didn't know better, I'd think you were starting to care more about the town and less about the big business."

"Can't I have both?"

"I guess. Within reason." She paddled, leading him along the shoreline until they reached the shortest part of the river, where she waited for him to pull up beside her.

Their feet touched under the water, and neither of them moved away from each other this time. It was progress. And out here, in the freedom of the ocean, she didn't feel the pull of her former life as much. "Okay, we cross here. It'll be easier up on your knees, but you can manage sitting, no problem."

He eyed the distance. "Ah, how about I go get my power-boat and we zip on over there?"

"Can't. Too shallow on the other side. You can only swim or paddleboard, or go to the other side where you'd have to anchor and swim, but that side is rocky and dangerous with the current."

He sighed. "Paddling it is."

She popped up on her knees to show him how, and he followed suit and found his balance before they hit the waves in the river. Good thing it was off season so there was no boat traffic in their area to speak of. "You'll have to paddle hard at the middle of the river," she shouted back over her shoulder.

Her upper body grew tired from the angle, so she popped up on her feet with no issue. Before she had a chance to tell Trevor not to stand, he had already splashed into the water. This time he kept hold of his paddle and managed to get himself up onto the board again.

"Don't worry. I've got this." He waved her ahead since she was already in the center of the Banana River and the current swept her away from the canal entrance ahead.

She managed to row until she reached the other side, hoping he was doing okay. Once across, she turned to find him standing and rowing like a pro. Well, maybe not in stance, but he was standing. He was adorable, the way he wobbled and wiggled to stay on the board and wouldn't give up.

She waited for him at the entrance to the canal. Her heart fluttered with excitement. This was the spot where all the important things with her friends had happened when they were teenagers. They'd come here for book club, turned boy gossip, turned life-decision-making chats. She hadn't been here for years, not since she'd taken her daughter out here for a picnic when her first boyfriend had dumped her.

The waves beat against the rocky shore on the exposed side of the island, but she settled into a sweet spot near the overhanging trees. He managed to reach her side, and they rafted up to each other, sitting at the overgrown entrance. "Okay, now you need to pinky swear that you'll never tell anyone about this place. Not even Dustin. I might lose my friendship membership for even taking a guy here." She held out her pinky, expecting him to look at her like she'd grown fins, but he locked his pinky with hers.

"I so do swear."

She blinked at him as if that would help her see him better in an emotional way. "How'd you know how to do that?"

"Sisters. Lots of them. I was the only boy. Pinky swears were commonplace in my house." He released her pinky but kept hold of her hand so they could remain together. "But I have a question for you."

"What's that?" she asked, noticing he'd put back on his serious expression.

"Do you really want to share this place with me? I know I said I wanted to see it, but if it's important to you and you want to keep it to yourself, that's okay." His thumb grazed her knuckles, soothing her into a stupor for a moment.

"I want to share it. Don't worry. No guilt here. As long as you never share it with anyone else, we're good." She tightened her grip so he couldn't move away. It had been over thirty years since the girls had sworn not to share their hidden oasis with anyone else. Certainly there was a statute of limitations on that rule and it had expired long ago. "You know, if you want to talk about your ex-wife, I'm fine with that. I'm your friend, and I don't want this to be a one-way thing. You have stuff to get through, too."

"Listen, that marriage might have been to the wrong person, but—"

"But it still hurts when it breaks up," she offered, keeping him from belittling his grief.

"To be honest, at this moment, the only thing I'm sad about is upsetting you yesterday."

"I wasn't mad at you." She studied the way his hand felt around her fingers. The strength and tenderness all at once.

"What is it?" he asked in the softest of tones. "I can't fix it if you don't tell me what's wrong."

She let out an uneasy chuckle. "You're such a man. You can't fix me like you fix a boat."

"I can try. That's why I was giving you space. I thought I'd made you uncomfortable yesterday."

"Yesterday?" She rose a brow.

"Yeah, you know, when you caught me…showering."

She laughed, this time with humor. "No. Well, yes, but not for the reason you think. I was uncomfortable because of the way I felt after seeing you. And then when you brought Houdini back to me, it was so kind and considerate. You're the perfect package for *more than friends*, but I can't go there. It wouldn't be fair to you."

"Because of my ex? Don't think about her. I don't anymore," Trevor said with such ease, she believed him.

"No. Because of my husband." She wet her lips, as if to prepare them so the words would flow without restraint. "Yesterday, I was going through his things. Everyone says I need to move on since it's been three years, and then I met you. And this was the first time I ever thought perhaps I'd want to. But how do I forget a man I spent all those years with, the father of my child?"

"You don't have to." He squeezed her hand as if to make her hear his words. "I'm not going to pressure you to do that."

"I know. That's not the problem. You don't make me feel like I want to run from you. It's just that when you asked for those zip ties, I hit a wall head-on."

"I should've never asked—"

"They're only zip ties. It should've been no big deal, but it was. Those were Joe's. How do I take something from the man of my past to give to a man of my future?" A realization rattled through her. It was never about the zip ties.

"I didn't know. I'm sorry if I asked for something of Joe's. I promise you that I don't want to replace him."

"You didn't make me feel that way at all. It wasn't you. It's the guilt. Or the fact that I didn't feel guilty, which made me feel even more guilt." It was her turn to squeeze his hand. "Don't you see? It wasn't the zip ties I couldn't give you that once belonged to him. They were only a symbol of the real issue."

"Then what was it?" He lifted his sunglasses up on his head, as if he had to let her see his sincerity.

"Me. How do I give myself to another man? I was his for so long. It should feel like a betrayal, but when I saw you yesterday and I felt...awake for the first time in years, I didn't feel guilty. I only felt invigorated and alive for the first time since his passing. It made me realize I had to face letting Joe go. Only, I don't know how. I thought I had let him go years ago. And I have, but I can't let go of the promise I'd made on our wedding day." She took in a stuttered breath. "I know it's not cheating, and I know you don't need this drama, so that's why I pushed you away. I'm not the drama type, and I'd never bring that to someone else."

He pressed his lips to her knuckles and looked at her with soft eyes. "I won't push you. Take as much time as you need. I'll be here."

"Will you?" Tears broke through, and she hated herself for crying, but she couldn't help it.

"I'm not going anywhere," Trevor said, as if his words were all she needed to hear.

"Joe wasn't supposed to leave me either, but he did. I know that sounds selfish, but one minute he was here and the next he wasn't. I don't think I can face losing someone like that again." She slipped her fingers free and lifted her chin. "So friends."

He looked straight at her and said, "No. I won't be your friend."

CHAPTER THIRTEEN

Trevor wanted to take her into his arms and tell her he wanted so much more than friendship, but besides the fact that he knew it could frighten her away, he thought he'd fall off the dang paddleboard again. "I don't want to be your friend because I think you're worth the wait for more. I'm not going anywhere. Joe couldn't help what happened. If he could, I know he'd still be here. And I can't promise nothing will happen to me, but I can tell you now that nothing else will pull me away. I won't vanish on you or leave you. You can trust me. I'm not in any hurry. We'll be more than friends, but only as much as you want to be."

Her shoulders dropped from her ears, and she let out a breath. "Thank you." She looked as if he'd removed a tanker ship from her shoulders. "I haven't dated in a really long time, so this is all new to me. Wind told me that if I wasn't careful, I'd be placed in the friend zone permanently."

"Ha! No. I won't place you there." He wanted to lighten the mood and get her to relax around him to see it would be easy and not overly complicated or stressful to be more than friends with him, so he took his paddle and splashed her with some water.

"Hey. What was that for?"

"For making me stand up on this board and cross to this canal when it appears as if there is plenty of water to get through here if I raised the engine on the dinghy."

"The water used to be shallower. It's been a few years since I came to Friendship Beach."

"Well, this place better be as magical as you say it is, or you owe me big-time."

She paddled into the canal that was overgrown by trees arching over the water. "Oh really. And what would I owe you?"

"A kiss." Oh, how he wanted that more than anything, but he shouldn't have said it.

She splashed him this time. "I'm not that easy. I was always told not to kiss a boy on the first date."

"Wow, it has been a long time for you. In case you didn't notice, I'm not a boy, I'm a man."

"Oh, I noticed. Naked, remember?"

Her words caused a heat to surge through him, and not from embarrassment this time. He pushed a low-hanging tree branch out of the way for them to paddle under. "Oh, I remember you watching me. Weren't you taught staring's rude?" She paddled faster, indicating that she was probably embarrassed, but he wouldn't let it go that easily. "Let's get back to the date part."

"Date?" she asked, keeping her attention forward and ducking under branches.

"Yeah, you said this is our first date." He nudged the back of her paddleboard, making it teeter.

"Ah, don't do that."

"Why? Scared of a little water?"

"Not so much the water, but that alligator over there makes me want to stay on this board."

He followed her gaze over to the cement wall that reached from the water to the grass line and wished she hadn't told him. Two eyes and a hump of a head peered over the water, but it didn't move. "That's not good. Aren't they aggressive?"

"They can be. Let's just say, don't try to stand up and we should get moving." She paddled a little faster and kept her eye on the gator across the canal.

The mosquitoes swooped in, nipping at his ears and neck. "No wonder no one knows about this place. You have to risk getting a foot chewed off by a gator or malaria from all the mosquitoes."

She turned the board around a bend. "Almost there. And trust me, it'll be worth it. Most amazing spot in the world."

The tree canopy opened up at the bend in the canal, but when they reached a small beach, she stopped, mid-paddle.

"What's wrong? Another gator?" he asked, although he wasn't sure he wanted to know.

"Worse." She pointed ahead. "Look."

He rowed up beside her and found a bunch of plastic bottles and trash washed up on the sandy shore and floating at the water's edge.

"It's ruined. How did this happen?" She rowed through the trash, pulled her paddleboard up onto the beach, and unstrapped her leg.

"I'm so sorry. It looks like ocean trash washed up here." He pulled his own board through the trash and onto the beach, thankful to be out of the murky, gator-occupied water. The other side, overlooking a lagoon, was breathtaking. If only they could reach it another way, but the jagged rocks beyond the lagoon appeared to block the entrance. "I can see what you mean, though. You have wide-open ocean on one side with protruding rocks to keep people from entering this lagoon, and on the other side the canal that is shielded by trees so it isn't noticeable from the river. It's perfectly isolated and beautiful."

"No. It's awful." Her voice cracked. "Dirty. It was once pure and clean and amazing." She shook her head, and he could see the tears welling in her eyes. This place had been so special to her, and she'd tried to share it with him. "Everything around me has changed. I thought this one spot had been preserved, but I was wrong."

"We can clean it up. I'll help," he offered, taking her into his arms to soothe her pain. "It'll be an oasis again."

She didn't push him away. Instead she cuddled into him, resting her cheek to his chest. He was sure she could hear his heartbeat hammering against his sternum. In that moment, despite the mosquitoes swarming them, or the fact he knew there was a gator out there waiting for a snack, or the brack-ish-smelling water, he never wanted to move, because that would mean letting her go, even if only for a moment. He didn't like that idea.

For several minutes, he savored the smell of her hair, which reminded him of fresh-cut flowers, and the feeling of her body against his. She slid from him but kept hold of his arms, looking up into his eyes. "You really don't think it's awful here?"

"No." He cupped her cheek. "I think it's beautiful, just a little sad at times."

She bit her bottom lip and scanned the area.

"What is it?"

She shrugged. "Nothing. I just thought you might find it

awful. Then I'd have to kiss you." She pulled away. "But if you think it's pretty, then—"

He grabbed hold of her and tucked her into his arms once more. Stalling for only a second to make sure she wanted what he longed for, he realized he didn't have to guess. She rose onto her toes and pressed her mouth to his. His body inflamed from one sweep of her soft lips, and when she deepened the kiss, there were no more mosquitoes, or gators, or trash. Everything around him disappeared. In that moment, he knew she would be worth any wait.

CHAPTER FOURTEEN

BRI DOTTED at Julie's neck with a calamine-lotion-covered cotton ball. "Mother, where in all of Summer Island did you go during daylight hours to get so many bites?"

Wind plopped down on the sofa. "She took Trevor to Friendship Beach. A fact I'm sure she wanted to keep a secret since none of us have ever taken a man there before. It's sacred, and no men are allowed."

"Aren't you supposed to be with your sister?" Julie grumbled.

"Taking a break while her husband is home. Besides, the rest of our girl power will be arriving soon. I can't miss the big reunion. Not to mention, you're the one who called me to come save you, remember?" Wind crossed her arms over her chest and put on a scrunched-faced expression, as if she wanted the back row to see her disgust. "Glad I did, since I found out you broke a friendship vow and all."

"It's not worth the promise anymore. There's nothing left of our special place. It's dirty, polluted, and gator-infested." Julie ignored the twinge in her chest.

"I know. I had to get you out of there. Or did you forget?" Wind pointed to her cheek, where a large raised bump from a mosquito bite damaged her perfect complexion.

"Trapped there?" Bri dotted Julie's chin with the cool pink lotion, helping dull the itch if only slightly. "Sorry I didn't answer my phone. I was…um…working on something."

"What were you working on?" Julie asked, but when Bri did a side-eyed glance at Wind, she knew better than to ask any more questions until they were alone. "Yes, we needed saving. We went into the canal on paddleboards, which we've done before. Heck, how many times did we swim the river growing up? But for some reason, a gator decided to hang there today. And apparently every mosquito on earth."

Wind huffed. "I know." She pointed to her cheek again. "Good thing I have a week before returning to normal life. No way can I risk a picture of me being released with this gigantic blemish on my skin."

"Why were there so many mosquitoes there during the day?" Bri asked, obviously not giving Wind the attention she was begging for.

"Probably from all the standing water in the trash and on the beach. The entire place was covered in plastic and garbage. Oh, Bri, it was awful."

Wind obviously gave up on anyone paying her attention from her position in the room, so she moved and sat on the coffee table, putting calamine lotion on her own cotton ball and dabbing her cheek. "I can vouch for her story. I know. I had to take Trevor's dinghy and motor over there, and then I had to paddle since it's too shallow to use the motor through the canal. That's how I got this." She tapped her cheek again, as if they hadn't seen the bite yet.

"And we thank you for doing so. I'm sorry about your cheek."

"Just tell me it was worth my sacrifice." Wind elbowed Julie's side.

She touched her lips, remembering how kissing Trevor took the wind from her lungs and the strength from her legs.

Wind gasped. "Don't tell me you've been sucker-kissed."

Bri held a pink cotton ball a few inches from Julie's face and eyed her. "Oh, no. I think she has."

"What the heck is a sucker kiss?" Julie asked, regretting her question the minute it left her mouth.

Wind shot up from the table, and Julie braced for a theatrical performance. "Oh, darling. You really are out of the loop. I should've chaperoned you two." She *tsk*ed and looked down at Julie with a disapproving shake of her head. "It's a kiss that makes you believe there are no more guys out there for you. That no other kiss will ever be able to live up to that one kiss. That you won't be able to sleep, eat, or function again without seeing, feeling, living that kiss over and over again. It is a kiss that suckers you into believing there is no life beyond that one single kiss." Wind paced around the room uncharacteristically biting her thumbnail. She mumbled, "Trust me, I know."

"You're insane." Julie swatted Bri's hand away and headed for the kitchen to make some tea.

"Am I?" Wind followed, snatching the kettle from her hands. "Then tell me one thing."

Bri joined them, and they both stood looking at her with narrowed eyes, as if analyzing every twitch and turn of her body.

"Were you just thinking about that kiss a minute ago when

you touched your lips?" Wind tapped her foot, and Bri leaned in closer.

Julie didn't know what to say. If she admitted she had been thinking about that kiss, they'd make a big deal out of it, but if she said no, Bri would know she was lying, so she snatched the tea kettle back. "You both need to get a life."

Wind left the room, grumbling something about losing her best friend to a man again.

Julie turned on the water and filled the kettle. The sound of the pipes squealing at least covered Wind's rantings.

A hand rested on her shoulder. "Mom, this is a big deal. I know how you don't like change and how you've struggled with moving on after Dad's passing. He would want this for you, though."

"I know." She patted Bri's hand.

"And as for Wind's comments," Bri said, "I think she just wanted more time with her friend. She missed you. And after so many failed relationships, I think she'd hoped to keep things casual and fun between all of you."

Julie remembered Wind's mumbling about the sucker-kiss. "I think I know why she's had so many failed relationships." She turned, eyeing the living room where Wind had disappeared to, and leaned in to whisper, scared of the Wind wrath if she overheard the mention of a name. "Damon Reynolds."

"You mean Mr. Reynolds, who lives in Cocoa Beach and went to your high school?"

"Yes, he and Wind had a thing back in the day. They were supposed to go off to New York together, but then, out of the blue, he told her to go without him. That they didn't belong together and he had other plans for his life."

"That's terrible." Bri took the kettle from Julie's hand and placed it on the stove.

"Yes, it was. When she married husband number one when she was only nineteen, I knew it was a rebound, but I couldn't get Wind to hear me. We drifted even further apart after that, so I wasn't around when that marriage broke up. Perhaps if we had stayed in touch, I could've helped more, but life happened. Friends grow apart when they are geographically undesirable."

Bri turned the knob on the stove, and the electric plate glowed orange in a matter of seconds. "Sounds like she's had her own issues. Maybe things will work out with Dustin, or maybe they won't. I can give you one piece of advice though."

"What's that?"

"Don't get involved. As much as Wind meddles in your life, she'll never let you into hers. Unless you want to lose her as a friend for years again, let her figure things out with Dustin and you stay clear."

"No worries. I learned my lesson last time." Julie crossed her arms and leaned against the old white refrigerator door. "Do you really think there is something to this sucker-kiss thing? I mean, it sounds silly and made up."

"It's not," Bri said with way too much authority that told Julie her daughter had the same experience.

"Who?" Julie asked.

Bri shrugged. "Doesn't matter. It's old news now. Happened right after Dad died, and honestly, I wasn't in a place to be emotionally available to him. We went our separate ways and remained friends."

"I'm sorry to hear that. Any hope that'll change? I mean, if he's really still on your mind…" Julie said, careful how she worded her question so she didn't cause more harm.

"No. Not at all. Trust me on that." Bri smiled. "You're good, aren't you?"

"Me? At what?" Julie asked, not sure what she meant.

"At changing the subject so you don't have to deal with your feelings. You must be who I get that from." Bri removed three mugs from the cupboard and set them by the stove. "Do you like Trevor? Do you see yourself with him a day from now, a week, a month, years?"

Julie held up both her hands. "Whoooa, let's not get ahead of ourselves."

"Come on, Mom. I know you've thought about it. You're not the casual-dating type."

The kettle whistled, so Bri removed it from the stove and poured the hot water into each of the cups before retrieving the box of tea bags.

Julie didn't answer. Instead, she dropped her tea bag into her cup and watched it steep. The dark coloring reminded her of the brackish water. How Trevor had been such a trooper through all of the discomforts of getting to the beach, and instead of making her feel bad once they arrived, he tried to make her feel better. He was a good man. A man who made her feel things she never thought possible to feel again.

The front doorbell rang, announcing the rest of the crew's arrival. Julie let out a long breath, but before she went to face her old friends and all the crazy they'd bring with them, she made a decision to say her thoughts aloud. That way, they were real and not a constant battle within Julie's head. "How would you feel if I said yes, that I can see myself with him longer than today? Would that upset you?"

Bri abandoned her mug and rubbed both of Julie's arms. "Mom, I want nothing more than for you to be happy. I'm a grown woman. I won't have an issue with you having a new boyfriend. It's about time."

Julie took in a deep breath. "That's good to hear. Then, yes.

Despite all of my issues with moving on and the guilt, my feelings for Trevor are growing. I can see Trevor in my life, now and in the future. He is a good and kind man who is, as you put it so eloquently, hot. For the first time in a long time, I feel awake and alive and want to live again. Despite it being way too early to think of this as a long-term commitment, I honestly can't see a future without him in it. Most of all, I'm actually considering my future."

CHAPTER FIFTEEN

"DUDE, you're insane. Look at you covered in bites and sunburned. Is that woman worth it?" Dustin asked, sitting on the sofa with his legs up on the coffee table and eyeing Trevor with a look of disgust.

Trevor rubbed aloe on his chest and shoulders, trying to alleviate the sting of the burn. Obviously the sunscreen didn't last after he fell in the water, despite being labeled water-resistant. He didn't care. Each ache and itch was worth it. He'd never experienced such a deep connection with someone, not even Marsha. Despite the seven years they were married, they'd never had a serious conversation. It was all about marketing, attending events, and schmoozing people. Not that they'd spent much time together after the first four years, since she'd had her big modeling break and flown off to New York and LA all the time.

"You're not going to do it again. Fall for some young, hot chick who's going to ruin you?"

Trevor didn't like the way Dustin spoke about Julie. "This

is different, and she's not in her twenties or thirties, even. She's celebrating her fiftieth birthday soon."

"Really?" Dustin's eyes went wide. "It doesn't matter. That's not the point. You just got a divorce. You don't want to settle down again and be miserable."

Trevor left his shirt off and sat on the edge of the chair so his back didn't touch anything. "First, I know part of you is saying this because you don't want to lose your wingman again, but I also know you're telling me this because you care. Regardless, I'm not getting remarried right now, so relax."

Dustin shot up to a perfect posture as if his words finally commanded his attention. "Right now? So you're already thinking about that?"

"I didn't say that. No. I'm not. Julie needs to take things slow. She's a widow trying to move on with her life, and I'm a man who had his heart broken, was lied to and used. We both enjoy each other's company, and honestly, I feel safe and I trust her. And she trusts me."

"You know this is doomed, right? This business, this new life with this new woman? I can only stay so long to pick up the pieces this time."

Trevor tensed. "No one's asking you to. I'm fine."

"Are you?" Dustin shook his head. "Then what are you still doing here?"

Trevor's temper rumbled inside like an approaching Florida afternoon thunder boomer, but he forced himself to remain seated. "I realize it's difficult for you to comprehend a man caring for a woman so much he's willing to work to make her happy, since the only thing you've worked at is moving on to the next victim."

"That's not fair." Dustin stood and grabbed an empty cup from the coffee table and headed to the kitchen.

"Isn't it? You have a three-month rule. The minute that mark hits, you move on before it can get too serious. You leave a trail of broken hearts behind and don't care." Trevor knew he was stepping over the line, but he couldn't keep it in any longer. "I care about you like a brother. That's why I'm saying this. You don't understand why I'm here, why I got this sunburn or did something out of my comfort zone to please a woman, because you've never been in love. Not real love."

Dustin slammed the cup down on the counter. "Maybe not, but I've also never allowed a woman to take everything I had just because she broke my heart."

"You're right." Trevor rested his elbows on his knees and lowered his head to take a breath and calm his anger. "Marsha was a mistake, a huge, horrible, decision that cost me dearly. But she wasn't the right woman. When we met, she put on a show, convinced me she was this nice woman with dreams who supported mine and that we could grow together. It was a lie. She only wanted me to introduce her to people at parties because she couldn't gain access to anyone working as a waitress. There were warning signs I chose not to see because I was so flattered that this young, beautiful woman who didn't want kids was interested in me. It was exciting at first. The perfect situation. I was caught up in it all when she asked me to marry her. And it all happened so fast." He took in a deep breath and let it out again. "No, I'm not ready to remarry, but that doesn't mean I'm not ready to care about someone."

Dustin flopped back on the couch. "I get it, man. It's lonely being single. Date Julie, enjoy your time with her, but just don't get too serious too fast. You think I'm only saying this because I miss having my best friend to hang out with, but I do care. I don't want to see you get hurt again."

"I won't. I'm older and wiser now." Trevor sat up and

looked at his lobster-colored chest. "Okay, maybe not so much wiser."

"See, this place is no good for you. Let's go home. Tear up that arbitration agreement and take her to court. At least sue her so you don't pay her that ridiculous alimony anymore. Heck, no judge will award her that." Dustin shook his head. "Man, just stop running and fix this so you don't go bankrupt and you can go home."

"I tell you what. I'll speak to an attorney and see what they say. If I have a case, I'll take her to court. But no matter the outcome, nothing will get me to return to Seattle. I'm happy here."

Dustin didn't look happy, but he picked up his phone, opened the screen, and tossed it to Trevor. He looked down to see Marsha on another news site. This time the title read, *Marsha Thompson Left at Alter When Groom-to-be Discovered Her Truth—Pregnant With Her Ex's Baby.*

"No, not possible. It's not mine." Trevor scrolled through the article. "You're right, I'm taking her to court. I'm not paying child support for a child who's not mine. We divorced over three months ago. There's no way. We haven't been together since…" He froze, the last three months flashing through his memory in an instant and settling on one night. His pulse raced. His skin went cold. He wanted to scream. "The night before the papers were served to him. Marsha came over. She said we'd made a mistake."

Dustin nodded. "I remember. The next morning she got a call from an agent and was gone. That's when you decided to come here. If you read further down, you'll see she's about three and a half months along."

Trevor didn't know if the sting over his skin was from his

sunburn or from the life-altering news. Either way, it hurt. "But I was told I couldn't have children."

"You were told that once, years ago. Did you ever think the woman you were with then might have been the one who couldn't have children and it wasn't you who had the problem? Did you ever have any tests run?"

Trevor thought back over the last decades of his life. "No."

"And how many women have you had unprotected sex with?"

"None. Well, Marsha, but she had an IUD before we ever met and kept it until…"

"Until when?"

"A month before we divorced. Something about having an infection and she had to have it removed."

Dustin took his phone back and looked down at Trevor. "Now you know why you can't continue with Julie. She deserves better. Because now you have no choice but to return to Seattle." He cleared his throat. "Ready to go home? Dad?"

CHAPTER SIXTEEN

THE FRONT DOOR to the cottage swung open, hitting the wall. Houdini skittered from the room, probably to his hideout behind Julie's bed.

Kat waltzed into the center of the living room, dropped her bag on the ground, and looked down her nose at the décor. "Well, I've seen nothing has changed."

Everyone held their breath—well, Julie did—and waited for the next comment to come out of the rich and famous Chicago attorney's mouth.

"Just like you. How do you do it, girl? I mean, seriously? I pay a ton of money to keep my skin looking this good, and you live in Florida. The place where people turn into raisins by the age of forty-five from sun damage." Kat dropped her coat and opened her arms.

Trace shot past Kat and wrapped her arms around Julie. "Thanks. We all wanted to know how you really felt about our quaint little lives."

It was a quick Trace kind of hug. Little emotion, but being raised only by a father and having no women in her life had turned Trace Latimer into a tomboy who didn't believe in showing emotions.

Julie looked around at all of them, her three high school best friends. They all passed glances around the room until Wind threw out her arms. "Watch out, Summer Island. The girls are back together."

They all fell into easy conversation as if a minute hadn't passed since their high school graduation. Julie had savored their friendship then, and she welcomed it now. Each crazy, pushy, outrageous one of them. Funny, she'd dreaded their return, not wanting them to push her into something she wasn't ready for, but now she was so excited to see them, she forgot about all her apprehension and listened to all their latest and greatest news.

The ease couldn't last, though. Trace cleared her throat and studied her hiking sandals. "I'm sorry I didn't stay longer after Joe's passing."

Julie eyed her little blonde friend with the courage and aggression of a bull shark. "No. Don't apologize. You came home for me all the way from Antarctica. I didn't expect you to stay. You had important work saving the penguins."

"Right, the Gentoo or Pygoscelis papua." A shadow passed over her, like something had happened during those days.

"Stop with all the ocean geek talk before Julie doesn't invite us back," Wind said.

"It's fine. And of course I'll invite you all back." Julie looked to each of her long-lost friends. "I hope we can all stay in touch for a while after this."

"I'm so sorry I didn't come back to visit more." For the first time since her arrival, Wind looked honest, without a flair of theatrics.

"It's okay, really," Julie said. "I should've tried harder, too."

"Maybe, but after we didn't come home the first few years that you invited us to holidays and spoke about our book club, it was up to us to make things right. I think we were all so caught up in our own lives, we forgot how important our friendship was. I, for one, was excited when I received Bri's invitation." Kat lifted her chin.

"Really?" Trace asked what Julie assumed everyone else was thinking.

"Yes. I missed my friends. My real friends. Not the corporate, tough-skinned types who can't pick a book to read if it means winning a case of the century." Kat laughed. "And I make a new vow that I'll come back more often."

Trace put her hand out. "So I vow."

Kat and Wind piled on top with their hands, and Julie followed. They all shouted, "So I vow."

Wind shot back from the hand pile and waved her arms. "Julie's got a new man."

The house fell silent, and then squeals erupted all around her.

"I hate you, Wendy Lively," Julie grumbled, slapping her forehead and collapsing into the nearby chair.

"But you love me, too." Wind tugged Kat down to the couch by her side.

Julie shot up so she could escape to the kitchen. "I'll get some refreshments for us. I'm sure you're all thirsty since you're no longer used to the Florida heat."

Bri stood behind her with a tray in hand already stacked with goodies. "I thought you young ladies would enjoy some cookies and milk while you played." She giggled and set the treats down on the table.

"You think you're so cute, don't you," Julie said. "My daughter here wants to pay me back for bringing cookies and milk into a study group here at the house when she was in high school. She's never going to let me live that down."

"Hey, I won't turn down a treat." Trace sat cross-legged on the carpet in front of the coffee table and snagged a piece of fruit.

"So I hear that this guy is so special, you're willing to take on gators and blood-sucking bugs to be with him on our girls-only beach." Kat picked up a cookie and nibbled on the edge of it.

Julie scanned the room for an easy exit but knew she'd never escape the conversation, so she plopped on the floor next to Trace, snagged a cookie of her own, and leaned against the chair behind her. "Fine. He's a guy who is opening a charter business. I've been introducing him around town to help him."

"And kissing him," Wind announced loud enough for all in the room and across the Atlantic Ocean to hear.

"*Ooooh!*," they said in unison. Even her own daughter was standing nearby, contributing to Julie's discomfort.

Still, the thought of the kiss energized her, and she thought she could run a marathon, which was hilarious because she could swim miles but run only a few hundred feet.

"Not just kissed." Bri touched the top of Julie's head. "Sucker kissed."

"*Ooooooh!*" they all said again.

"You don't even know what that means." She looked to Trace.

"Of course I do. And you are so doomed, girl." Trace gave a crooked smile. "But taking him to our beach for tourists to visit? That's not like you. So I'm assuming you definitely were sucker kissed."

"I forbid him to show anyone else," she said, as if that wiped out her indiscretion.

"Then you admit it was a special visit." Kat raised a colored, perfectly arched brow.

Julie had forgotten how stunningly beautiful her friend was. They were all beautiful in different ways. Trace had that sweet, blonde, blue-eyed girl-next-door look. Wind was theatrically beautiful and wore darker makeup that accentuated her darker hair and skin. Kat wore makeup, but more subtle shades that highlighted her features and shiny brunette hair.

"It doesn't matter. None of you know what it's like now. It's heartbreaking. Trevor said he'd help clean it up, but even with our effort, there is so much plastic trash, mosquitoes, and that darn gator, we'll never have our oasis back again."

Wind slapped her knee. "We swore to keep our beach a secret and that it was ours and ours alone to keep beautiful. Obviously we've all failed, so we need to fix it. Tomorrow we'll go clean out that beach. I'll rent a couple of small boats with outboard motors that we can raise to get through the canal. We can load those up, and then I'll hire a service to go spray the area. We'll get our beach back, girls."

"Can't I pay someone to clean it for us?" Kat asked with the corner of her lip raised. She never had liked doing manual labor. Good thing her parents pushed her in school so much.

"And break the girl pact? No way." Wind puffed out her bottom lip in that dramatic way of hers.

"But she did." Kat pointed at Julie like a toddler on a playground who had stolen her swing.

"She gets a pass this once," Trace announced, as if her opinion was law.

Julie liked the thought of working with all of them but

knew there was still the danger of the alligator, and they could be aggressive. "It sounds great, except—"

"I'll call some people." Trace studied the cookies, and as if she'd given up on her self-control, she grabbed a huge chocolate chip one from the middle of the plate. "We'll look into humanely relocating the gator since there are nearby homes with children and pets. It'll be a threat to the community."

"How are you going to make that happen? You Trace Dundee now?" Kat huffed.

"Something like that. It's what I do. Swim with dolphins, save penguins, wrestle alligators, and pull hair out of bitter old friends who make fun of my job."

Bri snickered and left the room. "You were right about them, Mom."

And with that crumb she'd dropped in the center of curious, rabid, hungry, attitude-flinging friends to devour, Bri hurried back into the kitchen.

"You get a pass on beach but not on trash talk." Trace dropped her cookie and folded her arms. "What did you say about us?"

Julie held up both of her hands. "Nothing personal, and nothing that wasn't true."

They all snarled at her as if she'd committed the ultimate sin: the loyal friendship betrayal. "I know, I know, we never speak about one another to anyone else beyond our friend group unless specific permission is given," Julie recited the old rule, surprised she remembered it verbatim after all these years.

It didn't alleviate the harsh glowers, though.

"Hey, remember. Widow here. I thought you were going to cheer me up."

"Not when you break the rules." Wind *tsk*ed.

"What if she didn't break the rules?" Bri peered around the corner, and Julie was never so thankful to have her daughter interrupt.

"What do you mean? How didn't she break the rules? She spoke to you about us." Kat rubbed her hands free of any cookie crumbs over the plate.

"But I'm family."

"Family doesn't have any place in our group. Our bond is more powerful than family relations." Trace tilted her head. "Unless…"

"Unless I can apply to join? To be a member of the Summer Island Book Club?" Bri wrung her hands. "I know this sounds strange, but I've always dreamed of being a part of your group. I never had friends like you amazing ladies."

Julie had to hide her smile at Bri's obvious use of compliments to get what she wanted.

"Depends. Does mama bear think you're ready?" Kat asked. "If so, we'll have to take a vote and decide if any new members are being accepted. In the meantime, you need to find the perfect book for the next meeting. That is the most important part of SIBCS—the careful choosing of books. We'll let you know then if you're invited into our book club or not."

Bri lit up, and Julie realized her daughter was serious. She did want to join. "Thank you. I won't let you down." She disappeared from the room, leaving the girls looking to Julie.

"So?" Wind asked.

Julie thought about it for a moment. "You know, that girl has only cared about how I've been doing since the day her father passed. She's the one who encouraged me to bring us all together, and when I didn't, she made it happen anyway. If it wasn't for her, we wouldn't be here now, so I vote yes. I didn't realize it until today, but I think she needs some friends right now, too."

"What say the rest of you?" Kat asked, the way she always had for any group decisions. She wasn't the president of their club or anything like that, but she'd been spouting laws and rules since childhood. A girl born to be the prominent attorney she became, and Julie was proud of her accomplishments.

"Yes," Wind said without hesitation.

Trace nodded. "Yep."

"I agree. So, depending on her book choice, we can officially invite her into the society. Of course, that will take having the book club meeting and inauguration on Friendship Beach or she won't be able to be admitted," Kat announced in her authoritative way.

Trace snagged her cell phone. "Guess we better get to work, then."

Before Julie could stop them, they scattered to make calls and arrange things. Tomorrow morning, they'd be working on restoring their past, and for the first time in a long time, she didn't mind looking at the years behind her because she could see a life ahead of her now. A life with the possibility of her best friends who had been absent for so long returning to her life. And a life that included getting to know Trevor Ashford. A man who had sucker-kissed her. And she couldn't wait for him to do it again.

CHAPTER SEVENTEEN

THE MORNING SUN ROSE, reminding Trevor of the way Julie looked when she was happy. He longed to make her life better, but how could he now that Marsha was the divorcée who kept on giving? Gifts he didn't want. Not from her. How did this happen? They'd been together all that time with no issue, and now this?

The glass sliding door opened behind him. "She's calling again," Dustin said in an I'm-so-sorry tone.

"I don't want to speak to her, not yet. I'm thinking."

"Man, I feel for you. This is insane. How sure are you that it's not your kid?" Dustin asked. "I'm not trying to be mean, but we both know how Marsha is when she wants something. If she's even pregnant, do you think it could be yours?"

"Apparently she is." Trevor removed the folded paper he'd printed last night as if he couldn't see it clearly on the screen. "There's a bump there. Trust me. I know how crazy she is about her waistline."

Dustin took the paper and then collapsed in the lawn chair

by his side. "Man, this is such bad timing. Believe it or not, I was rooting for you and Julie."

"Sure you were." Trevor gripped the plastic armrests.

"Okay, maybe not, but only because I didn't want you hurt again and I knew Julie had a lot of baggage to deal with. But never, did I ever, want Marsha back around. If I could change anything now, I'd get in that little dinghy and take on the sharks to get you to Julie and far from Marsha."

"Ha. You would never go on the ocean."

"Okay, maybe not, but not because I don't care. Just that I'm not getting in or on that ocean for anyone." Dustin shook his head. "Sorry, man. What are you going to tell Julie?"

Trevor crumpled the piece of paper and shoved it back into his pocket. "I don't know. If I knew for sure the child was mine, I'd tell her now. But I'm not willing to lose her over one of Marsha's games. I'm going to demand a paternity test before I acknowledge any rights to this baby." He sighed. "You want to know the most pathetic thing about this?"

"What's that?"

Trevor dropped his elbows to his knees and looked down at the ants crawling around the pebbles and shells on the ground. "I didn't even want to be with Marsha that night, but she said she wanted to try again, that she wanted to stop the divorce, that she'd grown so much and realized what was important. She was so insistent, but then the next day she received a phone call from the guy she's with, or was with, and she was gone. Papers were delivered the next day, and that's when I knew one thing."

"What's that?"

"That I had to get far from Marsha and her games. The woman has some power over men to make them stupid."

Dustin palmed his forehead. "That's why you gave her

everything and ran. Not because you cared about who she was with or the breakup."

"No, man, but it took me being here for a few days for the fog to clear enough to see why I'd left so abruptly. Now I like it here, and I don't want to leave."

"Then wait to tell her. Find out more." Dustin slapped him on the back. "I won't say a word to Wind either. They're all doing cleanup work together over at that beach anyway. You headed that way, too?"

"Yeah. You sure you don't want to come?"

"Let me think." He tapped his temple like he was truly considering his options. In a weighing motion, he held his right hand up. "Go over water with sharks to get eaten by mosquitoes and a gator?" That hand lowered and his left one went up. "Stay here in the air conditioning, getting caught up on work and then catching a nap." He raised his left hand higher. "Ding. We have a winner."

"Coward," Trevor called back to him as he headed to the dinghy.

"Father," Dustin said, halting Trevor in his place.

Dear Lord in heaven, what if he really was going to be a dad? His hands trembled.

"What, too soon?" Dustin called out.

"Eighteen years from now, when the kid is grown, it'll still be too soon." Trevor hopped into the dinghy and took off for the river, far from any talk about his ex and her lies. It had to be a lie. He'd always thought he couldn't have children after his twenties, when he had a serious girlfriend and they'd been together for years without using birth control. Yep, he'd been young and reckless back then, believing nothing could happen unless they planned it. And when they graduated college and planned to marry, they decided they'd try to have kids leading up to their wedding. When they didn't, things fell apart. He'd planned on going to a specialist, but his college sweetheart moved on before he could, and he spent the next two decades avoiding serious commitments. Until Marsha. But when their relationship started falling apart, he should've been more careful. As an older, wiser man, how could he have been this careless, this stupid? If he could have kids, did it have to happen with Marsha after all this time?

He spotted several boats near the canal entrance and realized he was zipping through too fast, so he slowed to avoid creating a wake.

A short blonde who appeared to be leading the show waved him through, so he eased into the canal, thankful to be in the dinghy instead of on a paddleboard. There were several other small boats with outboard engines up appearing to search the canal. He steered around and rafted up to another dinghy on the shore.

His heart double-timed at the sight of Julie. It wasn't because she was dressed in a bathing suit that accentuated all her curves or that her smile radiated from the top of a sand mound all the way to the water's edge. It was that feeling, the indescribable excitement that sparked when he saw her. It's what they spoke about in movies and wrote about in books, what he'd thought was a myth. Had he finally found the right woman, the woman who made him want to live every waking moment with the sole purpose to make her happy? No, he barely knew the woman. But wasn't that the point of the legend? That with one glance, a man was lost forever?

And in that next second, when she raced to the shoreline, he knew for certain he felt something he hadn't felt since he had a schoolboy crush. Open to anything, excited about everything, frightened of something—no, someone—ruining this promise of a brighter time in his life.

"Hey, you. Glad you could join us." She offered a hand to help him from the front of the boat, and he took it and her into his arms.

"Nothing would keep me away." And he meant it. Yes, things would be complicated even if Marsha was pregnant with his child, but he would figure out how to make Julie happy and care for the child at the same time. She already knew how to be an excellent parent.

She kissed him—in front of everyone—with such passion, he thought the sand beneath his feet would melt. When she pulled away, she blushed and eyed nearby ladies clearing the beach of trash.

One woman, with a sophisticated yet alluring green bathing suit, sauntered up. "I'm assuming you are the Trevor Ashford we've heard so much about?"

He reluctantly released Julie and offered his hand. "Nice to meet you."

"Kathryn Stein, but you can call me Kat. I need to inform you that this beach is not meant for the likes of you."

"Kat," Julie scolded.

"Likes of me?" he asked, worried that somehow they'd already discovered his predicament with Marsha.

"Male. You're the wrong species to inhabit our Friendship Beach," she said, as if a judge in a courtroom. "But we'll allow it for now. You know, to help."

"Thank you. I appreciate that."

Kat held up one pointed-nail finger. "But there is one condition."

He looked to Julie, who appeared uncomfortable but didn't say anything to make Kat change her tone. "What's that?"

"You swear, never, under any circumstances, to ever bring another person here. That includes for your business, or a friend, or another girl here. Clear?"

"As the water in the Bahamas." He tried to use humor, but based on her body language, she wasn't amused. "I swear."

As if he'd capsized her anger and let it float to the bottom, she reappeared as if excited to meet him. "Great. Now that we have that settled, come meet the gang." She ushered them to follow her to the edge of the trees. "You already know Bri, I assume."

"Yes, I've had the pleasure."

"Told you he was a gentleman," Wind said with a theatrical giggle.

"And apparently you've met Wind."

"Yes."

"That only leaves Trace. She's the one out there organizing the gator relocation project." Kat pointed through a break in the mangroves at the lady who'd waved him into the canal.

"She's your friend who works with sea creatures, right?" Trevor asked.

"You remembered?" Julie said more as a question than a statement.

"I remember everything you've told me." Wow, he sounded like a teenager trying a new line to pick up a girl. He'd never been this clumsy around a woman before.

"Riiiight. Okay, let's get to work." Kat clapped her hands and plopped her oversized brimmed hat onto her long brown hair and headed for the other side of the little island.

"Come on. We're on lagoon duty. There's some trash we need to finish cleaning up." Julie folded her fingers between his and led him down the beach to the other side. In that moment, he thought he could follow her anywhere, but would she want him if he told her the truth? It was too early in their relationship to face such an extreme situation.

Julie paused at the edge of the water and held both his hands so they faced each other. His pulse quickened at the thought of another kiss. "I know they can be overwhelming, but they're good people."

"What?" He realized he'd been in deep thought about his issues and decided he had to tell her something. "I think they're great. Everyone around you is great, even Houdini. And you're the best." He tugged her a step closer and touched his forehead to hers, willing himself to tell her everything and for her to accept him and all his drama.

"Then what is it?" she whispered.

He let out a seven-year-old failed-marriage sigh and inhaled the hope of a new beginning. "I'm afraid my ex-wife, Marsha, has created another media storm, and her waves have reached me once again." He lifted his chin and faced her, eye-to-eye, to tell her the truth. "I want you to know that I thought that all the drama was behind me. I'd left it and her back in Seattle, but she has a way of mucking the waters." He took in another breath, this one caught somewhere between his lungs and the truth. "She's creating issues, and I would never want them to reach you. I-I don't want you hurt in any way."

She leaned in and stood on her toes. "Shhh." Her lips pressed to his cheek, to the corner of his lips, to the other side of his mouth before she lowered to her heels once more. "You've been dealing with my issues since day one. My back and forth with guilt and fear and want." She blinked up at him. "Trust me as I've trusted you. I won't let your ex-wife run me off."

"But…" He opened his mouth to tell her everything, to confess the situation that could change things between them.

"Hey, you two. Back to work. You can play kissy-face later," Kat yelled through the trees.

Julie popped up on her toes again and placed a chaste kiss on his lips and then went to work.

Since here, in front of everyone, wasn't the right place to share such news, he went to work. He picked up trash and moved branches for hours alongside Julie. Chance after chance presented itself, but he didn't say anything. As the day faded, he knew he had to tell her the first chance he could, before she found out from Wind and her internet snooping.

With two bags in hand, he dropped them into the dinghy, brushed off the sand on his legs and hands, and turned to march across the beach to tell her they needed to speak, alone, after they finished.

Trace tied up her dinghy. "Gator's relocated. It's safe now." She hopped out and looked at Trevor. "Sorry I couldn't introduce myself earlier. I'm Trace Latimer. I was Julie's best friend growing up."

He offered his hand, but his gaze remained on Julie and the horrible task awaiting him.

"You know, in all my years I've known Jewels, she's never once looked as excited or passionate about a man as she does now."

He let out a nervous chuckle. "Except for when she met Joe, I'm sure."

"No. I mean ever." After dropping her info bomb, she waltzed away, leaving Trevor with a knot of indecision in his gut. If he could prove Marsha's child wasn't his, he wouldn't have to upset Julie at all. And he never wanted to cause her any trouble. He only wanted to make her happy. She deserved that, not the drama of Marsha. He knew it was a mistake, but he could only hope that he could clear up the mess before Julie found out about the baby. He didn't want anything to ruin his chances with Julie before they were beyond the starting line of their relationship. Who was he kidding? He'd fallen in love the minute he followed Houdini to Julie's shop that day. And when he saw her on the beach that night, she'd stolen his heart, and he never wanted it back.

CHAPTER EIGHTEEN

JULIE'S FRIENDS and Bri plopped down around her in her room on the bed, desk chair, and floor. Houdini skittered from her lap up to his shelf on the wall. Kat, dressed way too fancy for Cassie's Catch in her stiletto-heeled sandals and puffy-sleeved dress, set a gold box with a big red ribbon around it on the comforter. "Before we go out for stage one of Operation Jewels's Birthday Celebration, we need you to open this."

Julie eyed the box, unsure what her friends had up their sleeves. "What's in it?"

"Open it to find out, silly." Wind scooted the desk chair closer and nudged into Julie's side.

Julie looked to Trace for any sign of what to expect.

"Don't look at me. I wasn't involved in this part of the operation. I'm in charge of the finale."

Bri sat up on her knees. "I'm not a member yet, so I have no idea, but I'm excited for you to open it."

Julie eyed Kat. "You shouldn't have."

"I know, I know. We could save time if you stop saying

things like 'this is too much' or 'I can't accept this' and move forward with this week."

"Okay." Julie decided she'd shoot the level six rapids of their plans instead of trying to swim upstream and ripped open the box to find a sexy summer dress. "Ah, you bought something for yourself and gave it to me?"

"No, silly." Wind pulled out the dress—well, Julie thought it was a dress, but maybe it was a shirt. She leaned into the box and sifted through the tissue paper.

"What are you looking for?" Kat raised a brow at her.

"The rest of the material."

Bri burst into laughter. "This gives new meaning to the term hot mama."

They doubled over, sounding like a bunch of dolphins in heat—Julie didn't know exactly what that sounded like, but she imagined it sounded like this. "Seriously, you don't expect me to wear that someday."

"Nope. Of course not," Wind said, twirling around the room as if to make the dress dance. "Tonight, silly."

"To Cassie's?" Julie pushed the box out of her way and headed for the door. "No way. No how."

Trace intercepted before Julie could reach the door. "I'll even wear a dress."

"What?" That stopped Julie's escape. "Tonight?"

"No, I actually can't make it tonight. I have to finish up with the gator relocation, including paperwork and taking the guys to a nearby dive bar as a thanks for their help. But on the night of your big birthday bash. That's when I'll wear a dress."

"Oh, Cracker Jacks and all that is holy, now you've got to wear that tonight. How could you refuse a chance to see Tomboy Trace in a dress?" Wind turned to Trace. "That doesn't mean a skort, right?"

"Nope. I'll wear a dress." Trace released her grip from around Julie's arms.

Julie eyed the dress and then Bri. "I can't."

"Try it on." Bri stood up and took the dress from Wind, holding it to Julie's shoulders. "Oh, yeah, if this doesn't get Trevor drooling like a hound dog, I don't know what will."

"Thanks for the visual. Fine. I'll try it on, but I won't promise to wear it."

Houdini stood on his hind legs and chirped.

"Great, not you, too." She stripped off her shirt and shorts and shoved the dress over her head, tugging it down to a presentable length. Only, Kat came up behind her and yanked it higher and adjusted the straps.

She turned to gasp. Houdini covered his eyes and bowed his head as if he couldn't look at her.

"No way. No how." Julie tucked her fingers under the hem to pull the dress over her head and away from her body.

"Wait." Bri stilled Julie's movement. "Mom, look." She turned Julie to face the mirror, and to her shock, she didn't look like a beach bimbo. Yes, the dress was tighter and shorter than she'd normally wear, but it had a sophistication to it that screamed Kat had had a say in its purchase.

Julie took a step toward the mirror, turning side to side. The dress pushed her average-sized breasts into a thirty-year-old position. The straps weren't overly tight over her shoulders because it fit so well around her chest, so it didn't cut into her skin to cause the back fat flap. The color was unique —not silver, not blue, more whale shark than dolphin but with a hint of a deep ocean hue. "I will confess one thing. You and Wind are an unstoppable team when it comes to clothes shopping. This is sophistication with sass." She turned to look at them both. "I've missed you guys so much."

Wind didn't say anything. She only blinked at Julie as if this was the most shocking news she'd heard in her life.

"Wow, I think you stunned Wind silent." Trace waved her hand at Wind as if to pull her from a daydream. "Never thought that was possible."

Wind shot into Julie's arms and held her like a preserver in a life storm. "I've missed you so much, too."

Kat swiped at her eyes but kept her distance. "Yeah, same here."

Had her perfect friends who'd had fulfilling, amazing lives actually thought about her and her quaint existence over the years? "I didn't know you ever thought about me."

Wind pushed her to arm's length. "Are you kidding? How many times did I try to come back after Joe passed? Only to be told you didn't need me."

"I thought you were being nice, but you had a life in New York. You don't belong here in the sleepy town of Summer Island."

Wind pushed Julie's hair away from her face. "Oh girl, my place has always been here. If not in body, then in soul. My life has never been full without the three of you."

Looking into Wind's gaze, Julie believed her words. It wasn't theatrical or attention-seeking. Her tone was honest and pure.

"I had no idea. I've always thought my little life here was a letdown to all of you. I never wanted to hold any of you back."

"Hon, I'd trade all of it for the happiness you found." Kat joined them and opened the circle hug to Trace, who summoned Bri in with them.

"See, Mom, I told you that your friends didn't forget about you, because you're unforgettable."

Trace tilted her head toward Julie's body. "Especially in that dress."

"I can't wear this," Julie protested, but when the four of them turned her to face herself in the mirror once again, she had to see that she wasn't the old, widow hag she'd thought but still a vibrant woman with years left to live.

"Hair and makeup next," Wind announced, grabbing her ridiculously large duffel of tools and dropping it with a clatter onto the small desk.

Before Julie could protest, she was forced into the chair. After a minute of her friends surrounding her, it didn't matter what she wore. Even if they hadn't picked out the perfect dress, even if they had chosen a potato sack, she would wear it with pride. Because in that moment, she realized she'd never lost her friends. They'd always been there, waiting for her to invite them back into her life.

When they were done curling hair and lashes, painting lips and cheeks, and fluffing hair and boobs, they stood her up in front of the mirror once more. In that moment, she knew one thing. It was time to move forward with her life. Tonight would be the night she'd tell Trevor that she was ready to move things forward between them. That she enjoyed every minute she spent with him, and hopefully in this dress, she would hook him into wanting the same with her. She felt alive, excited, ready to take on the world. Nothing would thwart her now, and she owed all of this to her long-lost-but-now-found, best, lifelong friends.

CHAPTER NINETEEN

TREVOR STRAIGHTENED his button-up shirt and combed his hair once more, eyeing the small mirror in his bathroom. "I have to tell her now."

Dustin clapped him on the back, trying to see around Trevor's shoulder. "Dude, not tonight."

"I thought you were the one urging me to come clean." Trevor moved away from the small mirror, knowing that Sir Primps A Lot would never leave until he made sure every last hair was in its perfect place.

"Yes, but not when it's a celebration for her. That would be insanely selfish." He picked up his toothbrush and loaded it with whitening toothpaste. "You can't ruin her evening to unload your conscience. Besides, you haven't even spoken to Marsha yet."

"I tried calling her. After her fifty missed calls to me, I finally returned it and she didn't answer. That woman doesn't just play games. She invented relationship drama strategies. I won't let her ruin this with Julie." Trevor abandoned the bathroom and snagged his jacket. Despite the heat, he wasn't sure how formal the party would be, so he opted to take one in case. "This woman is different than any I've ever dated."

"I'd say so. For once you found one who suits you instead of me." Dustin began brushing his teeth with his electric toothbrush, so Trevor went to the doorway so he could be heard loud and clear.

"What are you talking about?"

Dustin kept brushing, making Trevor stand there waiting for him to finish so he would answer—or was the man buying time?

"You know, I'm starting to think you and Marsha would've been better matched."

Dustin spit out the toothpaste and turned off the brush. "Exactly."

"What?" Treavor harrumphed. "Did you have a thing for Marsha?"

"Dear God, no." Dustin plopped his toothbrush back on the charger and pushed past Trevor. "That drama dressed as a diva is all yours, bro."

"Then what are you saying?"

"I'm saying that she is the type of woman I would go for. The type a guy dates, has a fling with, and then moves on. Not the type you marry. That's your problem."

"What are you talking about?" Trevor held his coat tight to his chest, preparing for the insanity about to spew from Dustin's mouth.

"Come on, you've got to see it, man. Ever since your fresh-out-of-college sweetheart wanted to get married and have a family, you've been torn between *happily ever after* and the *happily for now* game. Dude. I'm a firm player in the now game, but you've always been meant for the ever after."

"Then why did I wait to marry till my forties? Huh? And to a woman like Marsha?"

"Because you were told you couldn't have children. When one doc told you that he believed you were sterile due to a horrible case of chickenpox as a child, you decided you would save that childhood sweetheart with the white picket fence fantasy from a life with a sterile man. You've avoided relationships ever since by dating my type of woman."

"Your type?"

"Yes... Fun, exciting, and noncommittal."

Trevor thought back over his love life. "But I did marry a younger woman who's pregnant."

"Yes. She told you she never wanted kids because she had to keep her body looking good for modeling. I swear the minute she said that to you, the ever-after compromise switch in that brain of yours flicked and you were racing down the aisle. You've been wanting a forever and settling until you could have it. Now, you might have more than you bargained for, bud."

Trevor fell back onto the bed. "You might actually be on to something." He'd planned on marrying at a young age and having a family. That's when he unlocked the door to his memories. "I didn't leave Sara after I found out I wouldn't be able to have kids. We decided to try for a while, and when she didn't get pregnant, she broke it off. She couldn't face not having children."

"See, you're damaged." Dustin grabbed his jacket and waved Trevor to follow. "Let's not add being late to your girlfriend's party to the list of reasons she should reject you. After all, you've finally found the right woman at the right time of your life."

That drew him off the bed, and he followed Dustin to the

front door. Outside, the world was hot and humid but with a refreshing island breeze. "So you're not trying to get me to leave anymore?"

"No. I'm not happy about it, but now you're not running *from* but *to* something."

Trevor took in a deep, salty breath. "Why didn't you ever point any of this out before?"

Dustin stopped at the crosswalk leading to Cassie's Catch. "Dude, I did. Like a million times before you married Monster Marsha. You wouldn't listen. She had her fangs in you so deep I couldn't reach you."

Trevor chuckled. "Yeah, I guess she did. Hey, man. Thanks."

"For what?" Dustin looked up and down the street but remained at the light, waiting for it to change.

"Being the best friend a guy could ask for. You know, despite your crazy and you trying to convince everyone you don't need anything, you're a good guy."

"Ah, thanks. I think."

The light changed, and they crossed. "Now, about you. Why do you think you're never willing to commit to anyone? What happened in your past to cause such relationship issues?"

Dustin walked faster and opened the door to Cassie's Catch. "Nope, no head shrinking me. I'm not the one with a pregnant ex while in love with another woman. My life isn't in need of examining."

"Great, now I sound like a Jerry Springer episode from the '90s." Trevor entered the boat-like structure, but he didn't notice the wood paneling or the large, restored helm or the twenty-plus people in the room. He only saw Julie standing in a dress that accentuated all her natural beauty. A dress that made him forget his own name. "Wow."

Dustin slapped him on the back hard, as if to jolt him out of his stupor. "I think you chose well. Good luck. Remember, mouth closed, compliments flow, and tomorrow you can deal with the trash. Tonight is about her."

Trevor marched straight for Julie, unable to keep away from her another second. "You're the most beautiful woman I've ever seen. Happy birthday." He kissed her cheek and whispered, "Good thing there's a roomful of people, or I might forget that I'm a gentleman."

She blushed all shades of passion. He took her hand and stood by her side until people began to drag her away for other conversations.

He and Dustin hung out watching a game on the television over the bar while she did her rounds at her party, but Trevor never took his eyes off her.

"You look like you're about to fall out of your chair like a bad stalker." Dustin shouldered him, knocking him to the side and almost off the stool.

"She looks amazing tonight, doesn't she?" Trevor mumbled as if he was still processing how lucky he was to have such a smart, capable, sane, and beautiful woman to date.

"She does. Just remember that before you fall too hard, you need to tell her what's going on. Tonight, you don't get to make any grandiose declarations of love for her, or you'll regret it tomorrow. Truth, then relationship. Remember that."

"Right. Although, I still believe there's no way that child is mine. Unless it's a miracle baby, which I don't think is possible, it's not mine."

"Just because you say it's not doesn't make it true. And the truth doesn't matter. If she says you're the baby daddy, then you need to find out for sure before you dismiss her. Listen, you and I both know she's a liar and would manipulate any situation to make herself come out on top. That includes raking you over the coals for being a heartless monster for not taking responsibility for your unborn child. How do you think Julie would feel about you if reports come out that you weren't there for your own baby?"

Trevor ran his thumbnail along the crack in the lacquered wooden table. "Not good."

"Right. So for once, listen to me. I know you think I'm only a player who has never been in a real relationship, but trust me, I know what I'm talking about."

"Someday, you're going to tell me who broke your heart."

Wind appeared with a hand on Dustin's shoulder. "Oh, that's a story I'd love to hear."

Dustin plastered on that faux smile of his. "I'd have to have a heart to break it."

Wind laughed. "Right, I forgot."

Cassie came from the kitchen holding a round cake in the form of a beach with four different-colored chairs and books with a label that said Friendship Beach. "This cake isn't just for Julie Boone. This is for the four of you to let you know how much Summer Island has missed the vibrant quartet of girls who always made things happen. You were such a big part of this town that when you all scattered, it wasn't just Julie who missed you. It was all of us."

Mr. Mannie, a woman—her short, curly hair a deep orange—they called Francine, and other residents of Summer Island nodded their agreement.

Cassie continued, "So, I officially declare the first Summer Island celebration of Friendship Day." He placed the cake down on the table, and the girls swooped in around him. "Even if one of you decided to avoid the party."

"Trace had to finish up with the gator, but she'd feel the same way. We all do. We have all missed you, too," Wind announced, looking at each member of the town before she looked back at the cake.

Kat kissed Cassie on the cheek. "Trace is working on the big finale, so she gets a free pass, but I'll make sure she comes by tomorrow to say hi."

Trevor remained on the sidelines, watching the small-town family huddle together and chat about the fond memories of their past. It was nice to hear all the stories, and Trevor felt even closer to Julie, as if he'd known her their entire lives but only now had a chance to be together.

Once the people began to fade, he helped clean up and found himself holding Julie's hand at every opportunity. The restaurant emptied, leaving only the four women, Cassie, Dustin, and himself. Julie pulled him to the corner near the television blaring the news. "Listen, I want to tell you something." Julie's hands trembled, so he kissed each of them.

"You can tell me anything." Trevor held tight and listened but knew he should leave before whatever she said could change tomorrow when he told her the truth. "But we should wait. How about I take you for breakfast in the morning? We can chat then."

"I want to be with you. I'm ready," she said too loud, too fast for him to stop or ignore her words.

He squeezed her fingers and closed his eyes, searching for the right thing to say.

She backed away. "I'm sorry. I thought you—forget it. Forget what I said." She fled, but he caught her around the waist and held her tight.

"No. It's not what you think." He sighed and willed himself to tell her the truth.

"Hey, isn't that your ex on TV?" Wind called out.

He looked up to see the red with white font marquee at the bottom of the screen just before the newscaster spoke. "Marsha Thompson's pregnancy with ex-husband Trevor Ashford is the talk of all the tabloids. Will he man up and take care of the child or remain in hiding?"

Trevor looked to Dustin for advice, but his friend only shook his head and shrugged. Before Trevor could stop her, Julie fled from his arms, his reach, and most likely his life.

CHAPTER TWENTY

JULIE SAT ON HER BED, still in her dress, with her face in her hands.

"Mom?"

The bed lowered at Julie's side, and Bri wrapped her arms around Julie. "I'm so sorry. I thought Trevor was a good man, or I wouldn't have encouraged this."

"It's not your fault, darling." Julie held tight to her daughter. "I didn't even know him that long. I'm only upset because it shocked me." She patted Bri's arm and stood, putting herself back together with the façade she'd managed to keep for so many years. She cleaned her face of the paint with one of Wind's makeup removing cloths, stripped off the dress, and put on jammies. With one glance to her daughter, she knew if Bri would ever return to her life far from Summer Island, Julie needed to make sure she believed her mother would be fine without her. She was the best daughter a mother could ever want. "I'm fine, really."

Bri took the dress from the chair and hung it in her closet, as if Julie would wear it again.

"You're not fine." Kat came in carrying two mugs and handed one to Julie.

Wind followed behind and handed one to Bri. Trace had her own and collapsed on the bed. "I know people. The kind who dump deadbeat men into the ocean where they'll never find the body. Heck, I can do it myself."

"With two accomplices," Kat said, despite her law-worshiping attorney ways.

"Make that three," Bri grumbled.

"There's hope for you yet, girl." Wind raised her mug of tea at Bri and then took a sip.

Julie forced the pain from her heart and focused on her friends. They all needed to get back to their lives at the end of the week. There was nothing for them here in Summer Island. "Listen, it isn't a big deal. I knew the man for like a minute. I'm fine." She took a sip from her drink. Chamomile with a hint of mint. It had been their go-to tea whenever one of them had a broken heart when they were teenagers.

"That's all it takes for you," Trace said but didn't elaborate.

Julie decided to stay on topic. She'd have time to deal with her feelings later. "Listen, I'm not heartbroken. As a matter of fact, he did me a big favor."

"How's that?" Kat asked.

"This was the push I needed to start focusing on what I really want. Bri's been encouraging me to go back to working on my art. When we were on Friendship Beach cleaning up yesterday, I was inspired."

"You're inspired by trash? You are a little different, aren't you?" Wind said, but Trace smacked her in the back of the head.

"Yes. I've been looking for inspiration to create something

happy and pretty like I thought a true artist would do, but that isn't my art. My creative process is all about feeling passionate about sending a message. After seeing the plastic in the ocean and the condition of our little corner of Florida, I realized that all those people out there spouting about climate changes and pollution are like white noise. It's going to take something visual to show how these issues impact us all." Julie paced. She felt the idea bubbling to the surface. "I've been looking in all the wrong places to find out who I was post wife and mother. Bri was right: it was inside me the entire time. I'm going to start working in the morning on a piece that I hope will make some sort of small impact on our local community. For us to make more of an effort to preserve the natural beauty of our beaches and oceans."

Trace perked up. "That's brilliant. I'll offer my services in any way I can."

"No, when the week's up, you will all return to your own lives. I don't want you spending any more time worried about me than necessary. I'm fine, so you can return to your normal lives now."

Trace scooted between Wind and Bri and approached Julie with a tense expression. "What if I don't want to? What if I want to stay awhile longer? Would you have me?"

Julie scanned her soft eyes—vulnerable, searching, lost. "Yes, of course. Any of you who ever want to stay here are welcome. That's a given."

"Is it?" Kat tapped the side of her mug. "'Cause it has never felt that way. I know I thought after I left that I wasn't welcome back, as if I'd betrayed our friendship for leaving you behind."

"No, of course not. I just never wanted to hold any of you back." Julie swallowed the lump rising to her throat. "I have always loved and missed you guys but thought you'd grown out of my friendship."

Wind shot from the bed and flung into all of them. "Never."

They huddled together, but Julie couldn't comprehend why any of them would ever want to return to Summer Island when they'd had such fulfilling lives. But when she caught sight of Trace and the way she bit her lip, as if to fight tears from forming, Julie knew there was more to see than she'd noticed. It wasn't just Julie who'd suffered the loss of their friendship. They all felt the pain of so many years apart. "How about this?"

They all wiped falling tears from their cheeks and chins. Julie grabbed the tissue box and passed it to Wind, who passed it on. "Let's establish an annual Summer Island Book Club. Each year we'll return here, no matter where we are in the world, and we'll have our meeting on the clean and maintained Friendship Beach."

"I'm in," Kat answered surprisingly quickly. They all looked to her for further explanation, but she didn't elaborate on her enthusiasm.

"We're all in," Wind announced for the group.

Although the sadness remained in her peripheral vision, in that moment she was focused on the uplifting feeling of her Summer Island sisters. The friends who swore they'd never be apart but got lost for a bit, but now, they'd finally found their way back together.

CHAPTER TWENTY-ONE

TREVOR HELD his phone in his hand, staring at the screen, wishing he'd see Julie's number. It had been the longest night of his life. "Maybe I should go talk to her."

"Not until you have answers. Let her simmer down." Dustin eyed his own phone. "I think the girls are plotting your death, so it's best you stick with me for now."

"What makes you say that?" Trevor asked.

He held up his phone so Trevor could see it. "Because that was the exact words of Wind's last text."

"Oh." Trevor collapsed back into the old chair, which caused it to tip and aggravate him further. "How am I supposed to get answers when Marsha won't even answer my calls?" He sighed. "I guess I'll have to get them myself. I'll schedule an appointment with a doctor here and get tested to see if I can have kids. That way I won't have to wait for the baby to be born or deal with Marsha trying to play games for the next several months."

"That sounds like a good idea."

A small amount of relief seeped in, but it would still take a while to find out, and he wanted to work things out with Julie now. "This isn't as complicated as everyone is making it out to be. I'll financially support the child if it's mine and we'll do shared custody. He or she will spend summers here with me and the school year with Marsha." Trevor shook his head. "That poor kid."

"What?" Dustin asked.

"The idea of any child having a mother like Marsha is difficult to comprehend. I hope the motherly instinct kicks in once she has the baby." Trevor pushed from the chair. "I can't wait any longer."

"You can't go to her house," Dustin warned.

"I'm not." Trevor grabbed the dinghy key off the hook by the glass sliding door. "There might be new debris washed up on Friendship Beach. I won't let that place get bad again."

Dustin smacked the table in front of him. "You crazy? There are all sorts of sea creatures waiting for breakfast, and you'll be the main course."

"Not anything I don't deserve right now." Trevor wouldn't give Dustin a chance to respond.

It was a clear day with little wind and no chop, so it was an easy ride. At the turn into the canal, he rowed to the beach.

There were several plastic bottles already hovering in the corner, but the beach remained clean and the mosquitoes were nothing like before. Based on the chemical smell, he guessed someone had sprayed the area. He collected the bottles and stacked them together on the shore next to the old broken chairs. They'd planned to fix and paint the chairs, but they looked beyond repair. Perhaps he could order new ones.

On the the lagoon side an old, sun bleached paddle board he could possibly restore, so he set it in the sand near the rest of the junk. When he was done, he sat in the shade for hours, thinking about what to do. Part of him was excited at the thought of being a dad, a dream he had long since buried in his past. But he also felt for the child coming into the world with parents already split with no hope of reconciliation.

The sun rose higher in the sky, and he couldn't help but struggle with everything. He knew sitting alone on a private little oasis wasn't the answer, yet he stayed. Perhaps he only remained in hopes of catching a glimpse of Julie so he could explain what had happened. If he went to her house, would her friends even let him near her? Even if they did, what would he tell her? He didn't know anything yet.

When the sun was high in the sky, he knew it was time to face everything, and even if he had to fly to Seattle, he'd resolve this mess no matter what. He piled the trash into the dinghy and returned to retrieve the board when he heard the sound of an engine approaching When it cut off, he knew it was entering the canal.

His pulse revved to high gear, his mouth went beach dry, and his hands shook. This was his chance to explain everything. He couldn't help but smile at the thought he'd see Julie again, but when the dinghy rounded the overhanging mangrove, it wasn't Julie who approached. It was Skip from the marine shop with Marsha.

He forced himself to remain there waiting for her, attempting to stomp down his temper. After all, if she was the mother of his child, he had to let his resentment go in order to work through their differences for the sake of the baby.

Even the thought felt foreign and insane to him.

The dinghy approached under the momentum it had gained while traveling before the engine was cut out, but it didn't make it to shore, so he waded out to get the line and tied it to a mangrove.

"Special delivery." Skip called out. "I know, I know, the girls think this place is their sacred hideout that no other people are supposed to visit, but STSB reached me with an order to bring your pregnant wife here, so I followed instructions."

"Hi there," Marsha said, as if coming home from work on any regular day.

Trevor forced a calm he didn't feel. "What are you doing here?"

"You didn't answer my calls, so you left me no choice." She held out her hand, waiting for him to help her from the boat.

"When you clean up this mess, call my Rhonda. She won't trap you or dump you. Good woman for a guy like you." Skip grabbed an oar and stuck it into the sand to steady the boat.

Trevor didn't know what to say to that so he only nodded and turned his attention to Marsha. "I've been trying to contact you for the last day or so," Trevor sniped, despite his will to remain cordial.

"Yes, well, once I bought my ticket here, I felt it best to wait until we could speak in person." Marsha stepped onto the sand in her impractical, fancy-heeled sandals, making him hold her upright with each step.

"I think you two can find your own way back."

Trevor wanted to shout at the woman and tell her the girls were right about her manipulative ways. He had no doubt she brought Marsha out here to stir up trouble. He needed to get her off Friendhsip Island and quick. "Let's go." He headed for the dinghy but she crossed the sand and headed for the lagoon.

"Wait, we should talk for a bit."

"Talk? I tried to call you. Why didn't you call me back?"

She didn't even bother facing him until she reached the

waters edge of the lagoon. "Speaking about a baby isn't easy over the phone."

"Finding out that you could be a father in the society pages isn't easy, either," Trevor growled.

Marsha bent over, holding her belly with a groan.

Panic jolted through him. He raced to her side, held her up, and placed his hand over hers on her belly. "Are you okay? Is the baby alright?"

"Yes, the doctor calls them stretching pains. Guess my modeling career's over. Which means there's no reason for us not to get back together. We can have a real life now. The one you always spoke about." Marsha took his other hand and put it on her belly. "We can be a family."

A splash drew Trevor's attention to the water. Three girls were in a canoe, staring at him. Trace, Bri, and Julie.

He stood there frozen in Julie's broken gaze.

Trace hopped out, untied the dinghy from the mangrove, and tied it to the canoe. "Want to be on our beach so much, fine, you can stay." She pushed from shore and headed to the ocean.

"Wait. You can't do that," Marsha screamed.

Bri shook her head. "And you brought another woman here. Shame on you."

Julie didn't say anything. Marsha flicked off her shoes and ran after them, but she halted at the water's edge with a crinkled nose.

Trevor shook off his surprise and ran to the beach. "Wait! It's not what you think!"

Julie's gaze transfixed on him with an I'll-never-forgive-you expression.

And he knew she wouldn't.

Ever.

CHAPTER TWENTY-TWO

THE WOMEN DIDN'T SAY a word until they'd reached the house. Everything in Julie's world had been turned upside down in an instant. "I was such a fool. To think I'd believed he deserved a chance to explain. I'd planned on sneaking off to his place after we were done at the beach, but now..."

"Now he's on our hit list." Trace tossed the dinghy keys onto the kitchen counter.

Kat eyed them. "You realize you stole that, right? Theft is a crime."

"You would say that," Trace sniped.

If Julie didn't know better, she'd think Trace was madder than she was.

"No. I'd say if you're going to commit a crime, be smart enough to get away with it and don't park it at the end of our street and put the keys in Jewels's house. I'd sink it out in the middle of the river."

"Why, Kat, I didn't know you had it in you." Wind remained at Julie's side, rubbing small circles on her back.

At least she'd finally found her breath. It had only taken

the ride back and the walk up the hill before she could manage to even think about breathing again. Okay, she'd obviously managed the act. She just hadn't realized it due to being completely numb. Now, though. "How 'bout sinking *him* in the river?"

"Mom, I didn't know you had it in you."

Wind abandoned Julie's side but didn't go far. She sat next to Bri. "You don't know your mother. She once put those roadblock signs up in Edward Wilson's yard with a message that said *Beware, Dead End Man Ahead.*"

Bri gasped but with a big grin on her face. "You didn't."

"Oh, I did, but he deserved it. The boy tried to seduce Kat, and despite the fact she was too smart for him, he told the school he'd scored behind the football field."

"Mr. Wilson did that? Is that why he's always avoided you when we run into him?"

"Yep, but that's not where the story ends."

"It isn't?" Bri sat forward as if watching a thriller at the climactic scene.

"Kat waltzed into the lunchroom and punched him in the eye. His mother was so furious, she came to the school to complain because her son was too gentlemanly to ever hit a girl. That she'd raised him with respect."

"What happened to Kat?"

"I marched into the principal's office and confessed to being the one who put the signs in their yard and told her why. His mother was so furious that she took Ed by the ear, marched him to the locker room after school, and, in front of all of his half-dressed football buds, made him tell them that he was a pathetic little man who had to lie because he couldn't get a girl to sleep with him."

"She didn't," Bri gasped.

"She did. That boy never spoke out of turn again. They called him Dead End Ed for the rest of high school."

"I don't think I would want to be Trevor right now." Bri chuckled.

Julie thought back over their childhood antics and realized nothing would help this situation. "No. I won't allow it."

"Oh, why not? It'll be fun to torture him. What will it be? Signs are kind of our thing, and we can go bigger now that we have money. I'm thinking of renting a billboard on I-95 that says—"

"No." Julie stood, smoothed the wrinkles on her T-shirt and shorts, and lifted her chin. "Trevor Ashford is off-limits. I won't allow you to touch him or Marsha."

"Why not?" Wind asked.

Trace huffed. "Because our dear, sweet friend would never cause a problem when there is a baby involved."

They all looked to her with understanding. She'd faced such certain ruin as a teenager and knew that she never wanted Bri to suffer for it. "A baby's a gift. That child trumps a small, almost spring fling with a widow." She eyed the shop through the window. "But that doesn't stop me from moving on with my life. It's time for me to work on what I want next. I'm ready. You ladies find something to do, because I need some alone time to work on my art." She waltzed out of the living room, through the front door, across the garden, and into her shop. Each step became more difficult, but she made it the fifty steps or so before she collapsed under the weight of the truth. The truth that when she saw Trevor's hand on Marsha's belly, it felt like he'd punched Julie in the gut. For all her attempts at moving forward and telling everyone how minor their moment in time was, it was more than that. It had been a promise of a future with love and happiness, which she'd given up on after Joe's passing. Now she remembered why. The pain of loss crippled her with emotion to the point that she didn't want to get out of bed, or run a shop, or face the world. In that moment, she regretted ever meeting Trevor Ashford and hoped she never saw him again.

If she did, she wasn't sure she could remember there was a baby that prevented her from retaliating, and she might just pull a Kat and punch his lights out.

CHAPTER TWENTY-THREE

Trevor tried to keep his cool with Marsha. "Get on the board. There's no choice."

Marsha huffed like a child. He'd forgotten how infuriatingly immature she could be at times. "There is a choice. Call the police or coast guard and have them rescue us, and have those women arrested."

"Do you have a phone on you? Because I don't." Trevor hated wasting time with the obvious, but he wasn't going to stay on that beach another minute. It wasn't his beach to share. "And the only way to get us across this river is to paddle. You'll sit and you'll be quiet."

"Is that any way to talk to me? I'm your wife."

"Ex-wife. Papers were signed and you've been paid to leave." He picked up the makeshift oar he made from one of the broken chairs and held the board for her to climb on and sit.

She crossed her arms over her chest. "Paid to leave? I deserved all that you left me. I was with you for seven years. Sacrificed my career for several of those."

His anger bubbled. She'd never had a career until she used him to make introductions to prominent people in the industry while working on a business deal for his company. She needed to sit down and allow him to get them to the shore before he lost his temper. "Sit on the board, and for once in your life, be quiet."

Her mouth dropped open, obviously shocked that any man would ever speak to her that way, but she did as she was told. After all those years of never raising his voice to her, he'd wished he would've put her in her place a long time ago.

To his relief, the old board stayed afloat and he managed to paddle with the board. When they reached the edge of the canal and spotted the dinghy across at the end of Sunset Blvd, she erupted in her normal prattle, demanding the police be called.

Good thing it was a calm day, or he would've been forced to listen to her complaints even longer. When they reached the other side, he was winded and exhausted from attempting to cross the current. Once he caught his breath, he checked the dinghy but discovered the key wasn't in the deadman's switch and it was nowhere to be found.

"What are you going to do?" she asked with a flip of her long hair over her shoulder.

"I'm going after Julie."

"What am I supposed to do?" she shrieked.

"Walk back to my house and return to Seattle."

"I'm pregnant," she stated, as if unable to walk a few blocks in her delicate condition. Based on his experience with his sisters, there was no reason she couldn't walk.

"I think you can manage." He set the paddleboard inside the dinghy along with the wood slat, knowing walking would be easier than staying on that board another minute with

Marsha. He wasn't convinced he wouldn't dump Marsha somewhere out there if she started complaining again. What had he ever seen in her?

"I'm so sorry." She slid her fingers between his and held tight so he couldn't pull away. "Pregnancy hormones have me all worked up. But just think, I'm growing a little human being inside. One who will be ours. One who will renew our love for one another and make things better between us."

He saw the desperation on her face, something he'd never seen before. "Nothing has ever been good between us," he barked and tugged his hand away.

Marsha quickened her pace to keep up with him. He fought between guilt for treating a woman who could be carrying his child this way and wanting her out of his life once and for all. He reached Julie's place, but there was no way past the three fuming friends at the front walk.

"Don't even think about it," Kat warned.

"Please, I didn't know she was going to follow me," he pleaded. "I didn't even know she was going to come here."

"Doesn't matter. You can't talk to Jewels. Not right now. Not with her here." Wind pointed to Marsha, and Trevor knew she was right.

"Tell Julie I need to speak with her, please. I'll come back." Trevor snagged Marsha by the sleeve and tugged her toward the beach path to his house. They reached the tunnels, and he swore he heard Houdini skittering through them, but he never saw any fur or a twitching nose poke out.

Marsha managed to get ahead of Trevor when they reached the back deck of his home. "Wait, listen to me." She held her palms to his chest to stop him. "You have to understand. I can't do this alone. When I found out about the baby, I was frightened. Oh, Trev, I didn't know what to do. I freaked out and did stupid things. My shrink says that I self-sabotage because I'm scared of being rejected. I thought you'd reject me when you found out, so I ended it with you. And when you didn't fight to keep me, I thought you didn't care about me anymore and that you wouldn't want the baby." She turned on the tears and stuck out her bottom lip. "Don't you see, I loved you so much, I let you go."

For the slightest second, Trevor almost fell for her explanation, but he'd heard it too many times. "You left me, not the other way around. You cheated on me and didn't have the decency to allow me to divorce you without a show. You manipulated the situation in the media until I gave you everything and left."

"You were never there," she accused. "Not really. I always felt like you'd rather be somewhere else than with me." She moved in closer, caressing his cheek and pushing her chest against him. "Oh darling, don't you see? I only did those things because I wanted you to fight for me. I wanted to know you could love me, too." Her warm breath caressed his ear. "I've always wanted you."

The soft touch and sexual energy didn't cause his body or his heart to respond the way it did at one glance of Julie across the room. Trevor grabbed hold of Marsha's arms, pushed her two steps from him, and simply said, "No."

She burst into tears and howled like a baby. "You can't do this. You can't abandon me and the baby."

He knew in that moment that Dustin was right. Marsha would never tell him the truth about the baby. If there was a way to end this here and now, he had to try. "Go back to your fiancé and beg him to take you back. Don't waste your tears on me."

Her soft, pouty-lipped expression morphed into brow-crunched anger. "What? You don't believe the baby's yours? I dare you to even say such a thing."

The thought of ending this now and not having to wait on tests results and doctors and to fix things with Julie made him pull a Hail Mary. He could let her believe he knew for sure already that he couldn't have children. "The truth, you mean? I can't have children."

She gasped. "What?" Her gaze danced around the yard, the ocean, him until she settled into her pouty lip routine again. "But I thought…"

"That you could use me once again? Sorry, no. I'm done being manipulated." Trevor stood tall, waiting for her response and praying he was right and that he could end this here and now.

She burst into tears and threw herself into Trevor's arms. "Oh please, Trev. We can raise this baby together. You can still be the father."

All the anxiety that had been knotting his muscles released at her words.

"If you ever loved me, don't abandon me now. I know I've been impossible, but when Rett left me, I realized what a mistake I'd made. It's you. It's always been you, Trev. I love you. We can work through this."

"No, we can't, and I won't. And you're going to fix this, or I will." Trevor waited for her to stop the sobbing and catch on to his meaning. "If you don't set the record straight, I'll tell the press that I can't have children and that you slept with too many men so you don't know who the father is."

"No, you wouldn't." She shriveled away from him.

"Let me be clear with you for the first and last time, Marsha Thompson. I will end your social climbing with one phone call if you don't fix the mess you've created."

She crumpled in front of him. The façade of Marsha Thompson and her attitude wiped away with the ocean breeze. "I'm sorry," she whispered. "I never meant to hurt you. Our marriage was good at first, wasn't it?"

"It was, but it hasn't been for a long time. The games were exhausting, and I'm tired." He watched her wipe her eyes and look toward the sky as if there were answers.

"I played games because it was the only way to get your attention. When we first met, you couldn't keep your hands off me, but then things changed."

"You left for a modeling career. Each time you returned, it was all about your other life, never about us." He rubbed his forehead. "Listen, we can talk about all our mistakes and rehash everything, but it won't do any good. We both know our relationship ended a long time ago. If it's any consolation, I'm sorry you're facing having a child on your own."

She shrugged. "I deserve it."

He kissed her cheek. "No, you don't. Talk to the real father. If he won't man up, let me know. I'll come have a chat with him."

"You'd do that for me?" she asked, her eyes wide.

"Of course I would. Just no more games," he warned, feeling like a weight had been lifted from him. Not only about the baby but for finally feeling like the door to his former life with Marsha was closing with the anger and resentment on the other side.

She smiled, and with a nod, she wiped her eyes and sauntered to her car with a back wave. "Still getting alimony."

He chuckled, realizing despite her moment of humility, she'd always be Marsha Thompson.

The sliding door opened. "I'm proud of you. I thought I

was going to have to come out here to keep her from suckering you back into her world, but you held your own."

"I think I'm immune to her manipulation now." He chuckled.

"How did you know she'd believe you about not being able to have kids?" Dustin asked. "I mean, she could've called you on it to string you along until she came up with another plan."

"Maybe, but I saw it in her eyes. The desperation to make things work with me. I knew then that she was only manipulating me long enough to figure out a new angle or she already had one. It doesn't matter. All I know is that I need to tell Julie the truth."

"Go. Don't waste time with me." Dustin shooed him off.

Trevor ran all the way to the shop, but it was locked. He pounded on the door, but no one answered. He abandoned the shop and went to the house where Kat, Trace, and Bri stood like Roman warriors in a human shield line.

"You're not welcome here."

"You don't understand. The baby isn't mine. I can't have children," Trevor blurted.

They looked to one another and then to him. "Doesn't matter. If she ever wants to speak to you again, she'll let you know. Until then, I'd advise you to leave before we do something that we might all regret." Trace stepped forward and tossed his dinghy keys with the red float keychain at him.

"I don't want to leave things like this." He knew it was now or never if he wanted a chance to ever speak to her again. "I'm in love with her."

Despite his declaration, Trace pointed to the front walk. "Leave, or we'll call the police for trespassing and harassment. Trust me, they'll believe us. We know the sheriff. Do you?"

He thought about ignoring them to prove how much he

cared, but when Bri cleared her throat, she said the only few words that would make him go.

"If you really do love my mother, then don't hurt her anymore."

He knew in that moment, he never wanted to harm Julie in any way, but he had. When he'd hesitated to tell her the truth, he effectively told her a lie, and that lie lead to great unhappiness. He'd come to tell the truth, and he'd done that. Even if she couldn't hear him, although he was sure she could with the open windows, the girls would tell her what he'd said. It was Julie's decision now, so he did the hardest thing he'd ever done in his life.

He walked away.

CHAPTER TWENTY-FOUR

BRI ENTERED the old storage shed Julie had turned back into her studio. It wasn't too hot this time of year, but if she was able to make any money at her chosen profession, she'd shut down the souvenir shop and make that her studio. *If* she decided to remain in Summer Island. Lately, she'd had her doubts, but where would she go? This had always been her home.

"Mom, I know you're busy creating, but you've barely been out for fresh air in three days." Bri approached with coffee in hand and a tentative smile.

"I'm fine. Actually, I'm close to being done. It's just missing something." Julie wiped her hands on her towel and tossed it onto the old sink in the corner.

"Really, can I see it?" Bri asked, stepping closer, but Julie cut her off.

"No, not yet." She took the warm mug and sipped the magical elixir that always promised a pick-me-up.

"You should get ready. The grand finale is in an hour." Bri

scanned the studio as if analyzing every container or color or brush.

"Right, sure thing. I'll come up and shower now. It'll be weird having all the girls leave, but I'm happy for them. When's your flight?"

"Don't have one booked yet." Bri headed up the path to the house. "Told you, I don't know if I'm going back or not."

Julie hurried to stay with Bri, who obviously wanted to usher Julie into Operation Birthday Finale. "You are, because I'm fine."

"Are you? Because Trevor isn't." Bri blocked the back door to the house. "Mom, would it hurt to go talk to him? You saw the news. The baby wasn't Trevor's. He never meant to lie to you."

"I know that." She studied the floating swirls of milk in the dark pool of coffee. "That's not why."

"What is it, then? Why won't you speak with him?" Bri grabbed the doorknob but didn't turn it. "I'm not trying to put you two back together. I just don't want to see you unhappy."

"I'm not, or I won't be. Listen, you did what you came here to do. I'm no longer in a widow's funk. I'm living again. I'm creating, so you can move on with your life."

"Is it because he didn't tell you the truth and you found out from that awful newscast?"

"No. It's because he took her to the beach." She hid behind the rim of her mug and sipped on the brew to hide from the world, but it didn't last and she had to come back up for air and to face Bri's sorrowful gaze.

She bowed her head and opened the door. "I know, Mom."

Wind swooped by and grabbed Julie by the arm. "Come on. Time to get you dolled up."

"It's a beach party," Julie protested, but she knew better than to argue and never had the chance before Wind shoved her into the chair and was wielding a hot curling iron. "You know, my hair will be flat in ten minutes outside. What's the point?"

"The point is that today is your special day and I want you to always remember it. Good or bad."

Julie held up her hand to block the approaching iron. "What's that supposed to mean? Tell me you didn't invite Trevor to the party."

"No, of course not." Wind returned to work, and they were left in silence until the front bell rang.

Kat called from the front room, "Julie, it's for you. I think you'll want to come see this."

Julie looked to Wind, who tried to appear innocent, but Julie saw through her act. "I'll get you for this, and your little iron, too." She went out to the living room, bracing for the impact of seeing Trevor Ashford again, but she didn't. Instead, she found Houdini waiting at the door. He held up a zip tie with a squawk.

"Not you, too." Julie knelt down and picked Houdini up. "I thought you didn't like Trevor."

Houdini nuzzled her neck and handed her the tie. Inside she found writing in black permanent marker.

You are the only woman for me.

Trace grunted. "You did hear that man say he loves you, right?"

"I know. But…" Something still held Julie back, but she wasn't entirely sure it was about the lie.

"But what? Do you know how many of us wish we could find a man who would confess their feelings, look at us, or even pay half the attention that Trevor Ashford pays to you?" Kat said with an air of jealousy.

"It doesn't mean anything when the man's a liar."

"Why do you think that? The baby wasn't his," Kat said, stating the obvious.

Bri sat on the arm of the couch. "She means because of the beach incident."

Wind joined the other three girls and sat between them on the couch facing Julie. "He didn't invite that queen of mayhem to Friendship Beach."

Julie snapped her attention to Wind as if she were the only one in the room. "I saw them. Together. He had his hand on her belly, and they looked intimately entwined." The words were bitter on her tongue.

"No. Dustin said that Skip took Marsha to the beach. I asked Skip about it and she claimed the SMSB line told her that Trevor had been looking for Marsha to straighten the mess out. Trevor didn't invite her. He'd never betray you like that."

"More like Rhonda wants Trevor for herself and sent her mama after him. Remember when she tried to foreclose on Trace's land so she could knock it down because it blocks her view of the ocean?" Kat went to her side. "Listen, if you want to get rid of his body, I'm your girl. Heck, any of us are, but if you love him, which I'm guessing you do, don't let him go. There aren't many men out there worth fighting for, but this one might just be worth it."

Julie twirled the zip tie between her fingers. "I don't know. It's too much."

Kat tucked Julie's hair behind her ear. "Of course it is, darling. Anything worth living for comes with difficulties. Do you regret the years you spent with Joe?"

"No, not for a second." Julie blinked at her, shocked at Kat's question.

"So, despite the pain that you felt, you wouldn't have wished to spend your life differently?"

"No." Julie looked to Bri, who nodded.

"Then how can you let a chance at love again go without a fight? You already know how good it can be once you have it."

"Yes, but when you lose it..." Julie choked. "It hurts so much you don't know how you'll take your next breath."

The girls closed in around her. "That's when instead of pushing us away to show how strong you are, you let us in and allow us to hold you up until you can stand on your own. Because from this day forward, none of us will be alone again."

She held tight to Kat, Trace, Bri, and Wind. They were her zip ties that kept her together. "You promise?"

"We so swear as members of the Summer Island Book Club to never abandon each other today, tomorrow, or in the future," Wind announced and held her hand out between them.

They all piled their hands on with an unanimous, "We so swear."

"As an honorary member and your daughter, I so swear," Bri added.

"Guess we'll have that decision by the end of the night, kid." Kat looked between them. "That is, if Julie isn't too busy for us today."

She threw her arms around them. "No, never again. You are welcome here anytime."

They huddled together for a couple of minutes with Houdini jumping from shoulder to shoulder, chattering at them.

Wind pulled away. "Are you going after that man or not?"

Julie headed for the door. "I'll meet you all at the beach."

She swung it open to find Trevor dressed in his suit, holding flowers tied together with zip ties.

His gaze was desperate and longing, and she didn't need to know anything else because she saw it in his eyes. He loved her and would never betray her.

"Julie. I'm so sorry," he whispered. "I never wanted to hurt you. You've been through so much. I wouldn't be here now if I thought I couldn't make you happy."

She cupped his cheek, "Will you accept my apology?"

He dropped the flowers as if forgetting he'd ever held them. "For what?"

"For not trusting you more. I got scared and didn't know if I could handle losing someone again."

He took her hand. "You won't lose me."

"There's no guarantees in life, but I'm not looking for guarantees anymore. I want you."

"You have me." He pulled her into his arms and kissed her long, hard, and passionate until the room spun and her legs went weak.

"Wow, that's a hot flash and a half right there," Wind called when Trevor released her lips and pulled her tight to him with a half spin before he put her back on her feet.

"I thought I was the only one who had those." Julie looked between them.

"Ha, darling. I'm not sure you'd know the difference right now after that kiss. You'd burn from the inside out either way." Wind fanned herself.

Dustin walked in and stopped short. "What did I miss?"

"Everything as usual, darlin'," Wind announced.

"You must be the no-good friend who gave him bad advice." Trace offered her hand, but Dustin didn't move. He stood star-struck in the doorway looking at Trace as if he'd found the pot of gold at the end of a rainbow after a good storm.

Julie looked to Wind, but she only smiled. Apparently she didn't mind. "We should all head to the party. Hey Dustin, you swimming or paddling to Friendship Beach?"

"Ah, beach? Like across the river? Um, no. I'm not going. I have to go do…something."

"Come on. You can ride with me in the canoe. Let the love birds take the dinghy." Trace grabbed him by the wrist and scooted out the door.

Trevor laughed but didn't let go of Julie. Not when they walked down the road or when they got to the beach. Not when they had cake and played horseshoes. He only let go when presents were being given and he had to slip away to collect his gift for her.

"Where are you going?" she asked.

"Not far. I have a present for you. Well, for all you ladies." He summoned an uneasy Dustin, who still hadn't calmed down since being forced into a boat by Trace. Not to mention the fact he hadn't taken his eyes off her or made any suave comment since his arrival. How Trace got him into the boat at all based on what Trevor had told Julie about his fear had surprised them all.

They both ran to the other side of the lagoon and returned, each dragging three chairs with them. Each colored in a different paint—blue, green, and red. "These are for your book club."

"We might need one more," Julie announced, eyeing Bri.

Kat tossed another log on their bonfire. "I don't know. Let's find out what book she chose for our club."

Bri looked to each of them and then held up one finger and ran to the canoe. She returned with a bag and pulled out

178

bound paper a couple inches thick. "You never mentioned any rules about what kind of book or if it had to be published, so I wrote one." She held it out for everyone to see. The title read *Sisters of Summer Island*. "I've actually been writing it for some time now. That's why I originally reached out to each of you. It was going to be Mom's birthday present. It's a story about your childhood. I wrote down all your amazing stories with some fiction mixed in."

Julie touched the cover. "Oh, sweetie. I didn't know you enjoyed writing. Well, not since you were in high school."

"I do, but I was too scared to try to pursue it as a career. That was until I saw how you overcame your fear. I have a couple of manuscripts that I've been working on, but I think this one's the best. With your permission, I'd like to put it out on submission."

Wind snagged the manuscript. "Only after I read it. You better have painted me as the talented, good-hearted, beautiful sister."

Trace rolled her eyes. "It is fiction."

Julie faded away from her friendship circle but not too far. Only enough space to allow Trevor to hold her tight but close enough to let them know they were always welcome on Friendship Beach. After all, Summer Island Book Club was where their hearts and friendship belonged.

The End

FRIENDSHIP SALAD RECIPE

Ingredients

- 1 (20 ounce) can crushed pineapple (with juice, do not drain)
- 1 (3 ounce) package instant pistachio pudding mix
- 1 (12 ounce) container frozen whipped topping, completely thawed
- 2 large bananas, sliced thin
- 2 1/4 cups mini marshmallows
- 1 (15.25 ounce) can fruit cocktail, drained
- 1 (11 ounce) can mandarin orange slices, drained

Directions:

1. Pour the instant pudding into a large mixing bowl.

2. Add crushed pineapple (with juice), and mix well. Do not drain your pineapple!

3. Mix in whipped topping. Stir in bananas, marshmallows, fruit cocktail, and mandarin oranges.

4. Cover, and refrigerate until thoroughly chilled.

READERS GUIDE

1. Julie was anxious about facing her childhood friends after so many years. Why do you think she was so nervous?
2. After being married for over half of her life, Julie faced living alone. Worse, she faced dating again. How do you think dating has changed from the time she was in high school to today?
3. Summer Island is a small beach community in Florida. Have you ever visited a beach area away from the tourist crowds? Did you find it charming or boring?
4. Julie's daughter returned home to help her mother move on with her life. How do you think you would've handled one of your children giving up their own lives to look after you?
5. Do you think her daughter came home more for herself or for Julie?
6. Have you ever been a member of a friend group with so many different personalities? If so, was

there a lot of tension and arguing or did you embrace each other's differences? How about in book club?

7. How do you think you would feel seeing an old friend from your childhood you've barely spoken to over the years?

8. Have you ever been around a pet ferret before? They can be the sweetest, smartest little creatures. Oh, and mischievous. Do you think you'd ever want one for a pet?

9. Trevor retreated to Summer Island to escape publicity and his former life. However, he obviously had a love for sailing. Do you think he found the happiness he was seeking?

10. Who was your favorite friend or neighbor in Summer Island?

Bonus Question:

Have you ever picked a Florida orange off of a tree and eaten it fresh? If not, you should. Trust me.

ABOUT THE AUTHOR

Ciara Knight is a USA TODAY Bestselling Author, who writes clean and wholesome romance novels set in either modern day small towns or wild historic old west. Born with a huge imagination that usually got her into trouble, Ciara is happy she's found a way to use her powers for good. She loves spending time with her characters and hopes you do, too.

For a complete list of my books, please visit my website at www. ciaraknight.com. A great way to keep up to date on all releases, sales and prizes subscribe to my Newsletter. I'm extremely sociable, so feel free to chat with me on Facebook, Twitter, or Goodreads.

For your convenience please see my complete title list below, in reading order:

CONTEMPORARY ROMANCE

Friendship Beach Series
Summer Island Book Club
Summer Island Sisters
And More

Sweetwater County Series
Winter in Sweetwater County
Spring in Sweetwater County
Summer in Sweetwater County
Fall in Sweetwater County
Christmas in Sweetwater County
Valentines in Sweet-water County
Fourth of July in Sweetwater County
Thanksgiving in Sweetwater County
Grace in Sweetwater County

Faith in Sweetwater County

Love in Sweetwater County

A Sugar Maple Holiday Novel

(Historical)

If You Keep Me

If You Choose Me

A Sugar Maple Novel

If You Love Me

If You Adore Me

If You Cherish Me

If You Hold Me

If You Kiss Me

Riverbend

In All My Wishes

In All My Years

In All My Dreams

In All My Life

A Christmas Spark

A Miracle Mountain Christmas

HISTORICAL WESTERNS:

McKinnie Mail Order Brides Series

Love on the Prairie

(USA Today Bestselling Novel)

Love in the Rockies

Love on the Plains

Love on the Ranch

His Holiday Promise

(A Love on the Ranch Novella)

Love on the Sound

Love on the Border

Love at the Coast

A Prospectors Novel

Fools Rush

Bride of America

Adelaide: Bride of Maryland

Manufactured by Amazon.ca
Bolton, ON

27902629R00116